Secrets in the Silence

Elizabeth Fuller

Contents

Chapter 1

Florence:

I turned over and slowly opened my eyes. Panic shot through me the second I realized that I wasn't in my own room, but in Eric's. Oh god, I was really supposed to leave last night, I thought. I must have drifted off to sleep without even noticing.

Eric and I have been hooking up in secret for the past couple of months now. In the beginning I was really disappointed that he never wanted an actual relationship with me but after a while, I came to accept it. I liked us the way we were now, although some aspects could be altered...

Eric had commitment issues, I could tell this from the very start. His parents divorced about two years ago and he kind of hated them for a while afterward because of it. He would sometimes open up to me about how his feelings from the divorce and I would help him out. I understood him and I came to know not only the cocky, overconfident side of him, but also the more affectionate and softer side too- when we were alone, of course. We only spent time together alone, never in public. Even my closest friends didn't know what we were both doing. The same went for Eric's friends too.

Eric was the outgoing and arrogant popular kid that everyone knew, while I , on the other hand, was the quiet wallflower a grade below him. We were complete opposites. But for some reason, I really don't know why, Eric and I began talking and secretly hanging out. I wouldn't say he was a playboy, but he was no angel either. Most of the girls in school wanted a piece of him but I didn't see what the big deal was. Sure, he was good-looking and confident but I would never pine over him like others had done. I was a pretty chill girl, if you asked me.

"Shit." I muttered as I rubbed the sleep from my eyes. I tried desperately to get out of Eric's tight grip he had on my waist. I really shouldn't have stayed last night. I liked staying and waking up with him there. I liked how he would look bare, his hair a mess and his eyes filled with sleep, but I knew that he didn't want to wake up beside me. He didn't feel the same way. I think he might be a bit weirded out by finding me here beside him this morning.

But actually, now that I thought about it, maybe not that much anymore. In the beginning we made it clear that we would never stay the night or cross boundaries the other did not want to be crossed but gradually we became more lenient with the rules we had made. I slapped his face gently in an attempt to make him open his eyes and wake up.

"What?" he said groggily.

I noticed the huskiness of his voice and his funny bed head. I tried to conceal my smile. His dirty blonde hair was sticking out in all directions and he only had one eye open. He released his arms from around me and turned on his side so our fronts were facing. His head was propped up on one arm as he grinned widely at me now.

"Where are you going so early?"

I glanced at the digital alarm clock that was always on his bedside table, it read 09.36am. I furrowed my brows at him, why isn't he acting kind of freaked out by now that I stayed last night? If I knew he would react like that I would've stayed for longer but I was awake and alert now. He yawned and stretched his arms out as I sat at the edge of his bed and put my jeans on. He grabbed me from behind and playfully pinned me to the bed.

"Answer me now Flo." He joked and tried to kiss me. I scrunched my face up in mock disgust and moved it away from his, avoiding him every time he moved closer to my face.

"Ew, you weirdo. Get off of me." I squealed.

"You weren't saying that last night." He winked at me, continuing to go in for a kiss until we both burst into laughter.

"Eric, your friends are downstairs." Eric's mom knocked on the door and made our laughter stop abruptly. He put his hand over my mouth and glanced at the door. We both looked at each other in silence, our eyes slightly widened. Then we quickly jumped up and began to get dressed at the same time, running around the room like a pair of crazy people.

"I completely forgot." He muttered under his breath as he threw on a shirt. "Tell them I'll be down in a second mom." He called out, never stopping what he was doing once.

"Forgot what?" I whisper yelled, trying to find my shoes and socks. I have to say, I was kind of freaking out right then. Like I said, I was a pretty chill girl but not right now...If Eric's friends found out what we were doing, I didn't know what would happen between us.

"We planned to go suit shopping today with Mick." He replied quickly. Oh there they are, I thought to myself as I picked up my socks from under his bed.

"But prom isn't for another couple of months Eric? It's only January." I laughed but inside I was freaking out. I only had a few more months left with him until he left for college. He had told me about his plans to move out of our small town right after school finished to go to school in Farebrooke, which was only a few minutes' drive away from where I lived now. I didn't want to think about us separating, even if we weren't really an actual couple. Because I knew as soon as he left for college, I would be kicked to the curb and forgotten. There were too many college girls out there for Eric to even think about keeping me close.

"You know how Mick is Flo." He called from his en suite before he began brushing his teeth. Actually, I didn't really know how Mick was; I never talked to him before in my life. I didn't know much about him, I only had an idea of what he was like because of how people talked about him in my grade. Along with that, I only knew as much as Eric had told me about him too- which wasn't a lot.

He was even more cocky and arrogant than Eric, which was hard to believe but true, or so I've been told. He always had to look the best; an example of this was going out suit shopping in mid-January for a prom that wasn't until the end of May. It was kind of funny actually. Mick was always serious about how he looked but never serious about anything that was actually important. I heard he was failing almost every class this year but I wasn't sure whether that could really be true or not.

"Could you hand me over my watch please?" Eric asked from across the room. I was so lost in my thoughts I hadn't noticed he was finished in the bathroom and was ready to go.

"Here." I grabbed it from the desk and threw it to him. I tied my shoe lace and stood up, looking at him with a slight smile on my face. His hazel eyes skimmed over my body as he pursed his lips together before smirking at me. We stood silently at opposite sides of the room, sharing a moment together before he said we should probably go.

He snuck me down the stairs and past the living-room where we could hear his friends. Once we made it to the backdoor at the end of the kitchen we both sighed with relief.

"I'll see you later." He whispered and kissed me quickly. We both heard footsteps and the sound of his friends calling him from the hallway. A look of panic appeared on his face before he opened the door and practically pushed me out saying a short "bye" and closed the door in my face. I sighed quietly and heard Eric's voice from inside.

"I was just feeding the cat." He said.

"But you don't have a cat Eric?" his friend laughed at him. I stifled a giggle at Eric's panicked voice; he could be so dumb sometimes.

On my walk to my house that was only a few blocks away, the morning sun beamed down on my back. It was a bright Saturday morning. Our neighborhood was kind of like one of those white picket fenced ones you seen on TV. There were always those gossiping housewives, children out playing on the street and business men husbands. I reached my pastel yellow house, it was a lot smaller than Eric's but it was still nice and quaint. His Mom and Dad were both big-shot lawyers while my father owned the small hardware store in town. We lived a comfortable life and I always had a good relationship with my father. This was probably because it's always just been just the two of us.

I unlocked my door and was surprised to see my Dad sitting at the kitchen table eating breakfast and reading the paper. The radio was on low and as soon as I shut the door, my father looked up from his scrambled eggs and the sports section of the paper at me. I knew by his expression I was in trouble.

"Florence, glad to see you've finally arrived home. Take a seat." He glanced at me again then back down at his paper, continuing to read the paper. I tried not to laugh at his attempt to be stern. I pulled out a chair across from him and sat down.

"Yes father." I joked.

"How was Emma's?" he asked. Nothing unusual Florence, he's just asking you about your sleepover you said you were having at your friends house except you really didn't stay there and you lied to him, I thought. Although I hated lying to my dad I really couldn't tell him I stayed at Eric's could I? Sure he wasn't strict about boyfriends but how could I ever explain to him the situation between us? I wouldn't know where to begin.

"Good." I stated, trying to avoid eye contact. His eyes were burning holes into my forehead as I waited for him to reply.

"How is Emma? Did you enjoy your night?" he smiled at me, making me think he actually believed me.

"She's um, fine dad. Her mother was asking for you." I tried to distract myself by getting up and cleaning around the kitchen but he turned around in his chair to look at me.

"Oh I know." His grin began to get wider and wider as he spoke. "Emma told me last night when her and Kevin knocked over to ask you to go to the movies with them." I stopped what I was doing, my eyes widening. "They said they hadn't hung out with you in a while but I told Emma you were staying at her house, staying the night just like you told me. It's actually funny though, how they really didn't have any clue what I was talking about." I was caught out now. The situation would actually be quite funny, if you weren't me.

I covered my face with my hands to hide my embarrassment; I knew now, he had an idea of where I was.

"Where were you Florence?" He said, a little more serious than he had been throughout this conversation. I knew I was going to have to lie again to him.

"I was out." I said , trying to buy myself some time to think of something.

"Where?"

"I can't tell you."

"Why not?"

"It's complicated dad." I groaned loudly. "I went out on a date." I blurted out. Whoa Florence, where did that come from? I thought to myself. I looked atthe ground, I felt a bit guilty for lying again to him.

"A date huh?" he gave me a quizzical look. "That still doesn't explain where you stayed last night?' he raised an eyebrow at me.

"I stayed in Charlotte's afterward. I didn't want to tell anyone yet because its only early stages. Nothing serious you know?" I tried to play it cool. Now I needed to ask my other friend, Charlotte to back me up if I ever needed it about this. "I'm sorry Dad." This was something I really meant, I hated lying to him.

"It's okay hunny, just don't let it happen again." his expression softened now.

"I wont." I tried to fake a smile for him.

My guess was that he was still suspicious but he didn't question me anymore. I'd have to deal with my lie about my made up date later. Now, I had to get ready for whatever crazy plans my friends would make for us today, note the sarcasm.

I walked upstairs to my room and as soon as I closed my door I jumped on my bed and turned my phone on again, it had been off since last night. I rolled my eyes as all of my missed calls and messages came through from Kevin and Emma. How was I going to get myself out of this hole? My two best friends could be so nosey and demanding sometimes, always looking for gossip and "scandalous" news.

Emma: Where were you last night? We're both dying to know, you better spill;):)

Sometimes this secret thing was more hassle than it was worth, I hated keeping things from my friends. What was I supposed to do now? I really needed to talk to Eric about all of this.

Chapter 2

F lorence:

I texted Charlotte before I replied to my other friends. I needed her to pretend I stayed at her house last night before Emma and Kevin got any other ideas. If I was honest, I really didn't mind telling them about Eric and I, I trusted them enough to not blab their mouths to everyone, even if I knew it was very hard for them to do sometimes. It wasn't me that didn't want to tell our friends, it was Eric.

I always wondered why he was so secretive about it. I mean, he knew by now I understood he didn't want a relationship didn't he? Was there something wrong with me? Was he embarrassed by me? Why was it always on his terms? These were the questions running through my mind as the water cascaded down my body in the shower. I was getting myself riled up for no reason, I knew I would never ask Eric any of the things I wanted to, I didn't want to seem needy or like I cared that much.

I finished in the shower and checked my phone again. Emma had called me twice since I had left my room to go and shower. I rolled my eyes and smiled. She really needs to calm down, I thought to myself. I got changed into a pair of jeans, a baggy sweatshirt and my converse before attempting to throw my messy brown hair into a pony tail. I always like to keep my hair just below my shoulders but it had grown out a little, still not enough to put up without little strands of hair falling out. I pinned them back up and grabbed my phone to call Emma.

"Hey!" she said as soon as she answered. I winced at her loudness, holding the phone a bit father from my ear for a second.

"Hello Emma." I said unenthusiastically.

"Were going to the mall for lunch. Meet us there in a half an hour. That is, unless you have other plans like you did last night. You better tell us everything Florence." She said brightly without taking a breath. I laughed lightly at her.

"There's nothing to tell. I'll see you there." I hung up before she could begin to rant on about something else.

I looked at myself quickly in the mirror one last time before grabbing my phone and money. Fetching my car keys from the bowl on the kitchen island and heading out the door, I quickly said goodbye to my dad and made my way to the mall.

The drive was quick but it felt like forever when my thoughts about Eric tumbled around in my mind, I really needed to stop but I just couldn't. I was trying to weigh up my options but there really wasn't many. I didn't want to think about it anymore because I felt some uncertainty about the whole situation, I really needed to have a talk with Eric.

I parked my car and found Emma, Kevin and Charlotte waiting at the entrance of the mall for me. We headed straight for the food court. It wasn't until I sitting there with my meatball marinara sub that I realized how hungry I actually was, I hadn't eaten anything today. Charlotte sat down across from me and looked around, probably trying to find Kevin and Emma. I tucked in without saying a word.

"Hungry?" she asked me, her signature dark eyeliner made her hazel eyes to pop.

"Mmm." I attempted to talk with a mouthful of my sandwich in my mouth. I noticed she was trying to find the words to talk, which was unusual for Charlotte.

She was always very straight with everyone, she didn't care about offending anyone and she just told us to deal with it. Sometimes she could come across as cold but she was just a strong minded and opinionated girl, she was sweeter with us too because of course, we were her friends. She looked down at her plate and then back up at me again, opening and closing her mouth like she couldn't get the words out.

"So why am I lying for you?" she finally spoke. I felt uncomfortable now, I didn't know what to say.

"I was out last night and I don't want anyone to know where I was."

"Why?" she asked quickly.

"I- I just, oh Charlotte it's so confusing right now. I really hate lying and my mind just can't stop thinking about everything even though I want it to stop. I want to tell you three all about it but I can't." I finally blurted out, avoiding eye contact with her.

"It's okay." She said, trying to be soothing but I knew she was bad at this kind of stuff sometimes, emotions. "Why can't you tell us?" she added.

"I just can't, not right now." Our conversation stopped completely then, because we could hear Emma and Kevin coming towards our table.

Emma was an overly enthusiastic but sweet girl; she was this big character and was always so care-free, happy and just so over-joyed with everything. Kevin was like the male version of Emma, he was also very camp and he could be a little bitchy at times but he was still an amazing friend. The two paired together were even louder than when they were on their own which was hard to believe. They plopped their trays down on the table and sat down either side of me.

"So..." Kevin smacked his hands together and smiled very brightly at me with wide, excited eyes. "Where were you last night?" he said.

"I stayed at Charlotte's." I said, trying to sound convincing before eating another bite of my sub.

"Oh thanks for the invite Charlotte." He looked at Charlotte in the corner of his eye. She kept her usual bored expression on her face.

"No problem." She said sarcastically. We continued to chat and catch up while eating our lunch until I seen a familiar face from the corner of my eye. I turned around and seen Eric and his friends coming our way. He glanced at me casually and then looked away not saying anything. They were still a good bit away from us. I looked away and continued talking to Emma animatedly telling us about how she finally bought this pair of shoes she'd been wanting for ages when a voice interrupted our conversation.

"Hey! Charlotte!" a guy called that was standing beside Eric. We all turned our heads to see him waving his arm uncontrollably at her. Her cheeks flushed a light pink color and she gave him a wave back, laughing softly at him. He walked quickly over to our table and stood beside her, the group of boys following behind.

"Hey." She said quietly, it was unusual for her to be shy around anyone, maybe she liked him.

"How's it going?" he smiled widely at her, showing his perfect white teeth.

"I'm good, how about you Evan?" she smiled back.

"I'm fine, hey I was just wondering whether you wanted to come to our party next Saturday? You can all come too if you want?" he looked around the table at all of this. This guy seems way too nice to be hanging around with the jocks, I thought.

"Um, sure." She smiled, I looked at how is expression changed quickly, he was so happy with her answer, he was genuinely delighted.

"Great-" he began but was cut off.

"Evan, hurry up we have places to be." Mick called out in a bored tone.

"Well, I'll see you." He said goodbye and then left with the group. The table was silent for a minute until we knew they were not in earshot.

"Sooo..." Kevin said in the same tone he used with me a while ago, except maybe a little more excited. He looked straight at Charlotte and grinned. "Who's the hunk?" Charlotte went even pinker now.

"Because I'm with Grade 12 photography, I'm in his class. We got talking, he's actually really nice. He doesn't seem like the rest of his friends." She said, a bit more quiet than she usually is.

"You like him. I can tell." Emma smiled at her.

"Do not." She tried to lie. The pair continued to quiz her about Evan. I was happy for her really; I just sometimes wished Eric would pay be more attention when we see each other out like Evan had done with her. I wasn't the type of girl who fed off of boys' attention but was even a smile and a "Hey" too much to ask from him sometimes? He didn't have to act like we were complete strangers. That's just the way it is Florence, you knew it would be like this from the start, I thought. I wasn't supposed to care, it wouldn't make any difference anyway. Just then, my phone pinged and I quickly looked at the message.

Eric: Hey, want to hang out tonight?

My expression sank, I really didn't know what to do. I wanted to see him but I also wanted to talk to him about everything and maybe tonight wasn't the time or place, I needed to get my mind off of him for a while so declining might be the better option. I wish I could just ask advice from my friends, but I knew better. I sighed to myself, staring blankly at the screen now, trying to make up my mind.

Chapter 3

Florence:

"Hey, Florence?"

"Florence? Hellooo?" Kevin waved a hand in front of my face.

"What? Um, sorry." I snapped out of my daze and looked up from my screen to three sets of confused eyes.

"Are you okay?" Charlotte asked, her brows knitting together.

"Yeah, yeah I'm fine. What were you saying?" I replied, putting my phone away. I knew ignoring Eric was the cowardly thing to do but I just didn't want to have to make up my mind yet.

"We were just talking about that party on Saturday." Charlotte replied.

"Oh." My mind was still somewhere else. Focus Florence focus please, I thought.

"So will you come with me?" she asked.

"What about Emma and Kevin?" I wondered.

"I'm going to be busy." Emma replied, I knew it was a lie though. She could be outgoing and talk to anyone but I knew that this party was not her scene at all; she didn't like any of the people hosting it so she would definitely not go.

"I'd rather not." Kevin replied using a bitchy tone, holding his hand up and causing Emma to giggle. I knew he wasn't fond of Eric and his friends either. Charlotte made a face at me discreetly, silently begging me to say yes.

"Maybe." I finally decided. I didn't want to go but I would think about it because I knew Charlotte wanted to go.

"C'mon Florence, please." She begged.

"I don't know." I wondered what was holding me back. I never usually go to parties. That's because you're never invited to any, I thought. The idea of me having to pretend I didn't know Eric played in my mind, because he would definitely be there. He was the partying type.

Strangely enough, Charlotte left it there and didn't talk about it all weekend. We ended up going home from the mall and then staying in Emma's house that night, this time for real.

I never replied to Eric because I had forgotten about it until I was on my way home from Emma's on Sunday morning and seen him jogging down the street in workout gear. Oh shit, I thought, I really should've texted him back yesturday.

It was still very early, maybe around seven and the sun had just risen. I left Charlotte, Kevin and Emma still sleeping because I really just felt like going home, I hadn't slept in my own bed all weekend. His tall frame and broad shoulders made me look just a little longer as I passed him in my car before turning into my small driveway and parking. He had reached the sidewalk outside my house by the time I shut my car door. He stopped and caught his breath.

"Hey." He waved at me and smiled, flashing his straight white teeth.

"Hey." I said, grabbing my stuff from the passenger side and walked slowly towards my door but I stopped when I heard his voice again.

"Wait." He said, his dark brows knitted in confusion, like he didn't know what he was going to say. His green eyes looked me up and down. He looked annoyed for a second but then changed his expression again. "Did you get my text?" I was surprised that he asked me about it, I'm sure he found better plans for last night anyway so I tried my best not to feel bad.

"Oh, um, my phone was off I'm sorry." I lied. "Is something wrong?" I asked.

"Oh no, it's fine. It doesn't matter now." He looked hurt for a moment and quickly hid it again.

"Well, I'll see you." I smiled at him and walked in my door now. I felt slightly awkward around him, I hadn't felt like there was nothing to say to him since we first met. Usually the conversation flowed smoothly and we could just talk and talk for hours on end but something was different whether it was just me or it was also him, it wasn't the same today. Would it be like that whenever I talked to him now? I tried to put off thinking about it for another while; it was all too much for my sleep-deprived brain to take. So I went back to bed and forgot about my thoughts of Eric.

The week in school after the weekend ticked by slowly, I really thought it would never end. I usually don't mind school that much; I kept my head down, got on with it and got the good grades I wanted. Every time I seen Eric in the cafeteria or passed him by in the hall, it was the way it had always been, we ignored each other like we both did at the mall that day. He texted me on Monday and Wednesday, both days I ignored his text. I knew I was being a coward and I knew I wouldn't like it if Eric done that on me. He never ignored my messages, but I just didn't want to have to deal with thinking about what we had going on between us. I wondered why it wasn't until now that I started to feel like this. Was I making a big deal out of nothing? Was it just a phase? I hoped so anyway...

By Thursday, I didn't want to admit to myself that I kind of missed him. I was making my way to the library for my free period when a hand covered my mouth and grabbed my waist, spinning me around and putting my back against the row of lockers that lined the empty halls. I took a while longer to sort out my stuff in my locker to bring with me to the library so everyone was already gone to class. I opened my eyes to find Eric smiling crookedly at me.

"Hey." He spoke softly before kissing me passionately on the lips then trailing kisses down my neck before I pulled him in again and locked my lips on his. "God I missed you." He smiled into the kiss and rested his forehead on mine. I tried not to act so surprised at his words. He spoke genuinely but he had never really said anything like that to me before. He was never very open about his feelings for so I began to feel he didn't have any. I tried to figure out if he was joking or not when he chuckled lightly at me, out lips still centimetres apart. "Why are you looking like that?" he asked.

"No reason." I smiled back at him now. I played with his messy blonde hair but stopped as soon as he spoke again.

"Why have you been avoiding me?" he asked, I could see the confusion in his eyes and even though I had forgotten about how awkward our encounter during the weekend had been, I quickly remember now and took a step back from him.

"I just, I've been thinking..." I trailed off, trying to find the words. He looked at me with hopeful eyes. "It's nothing really. I've just been busy." I knew I was chickening out but I wanted things to go back to normal with Eric, even just for a little while longer. So I decided I would hold off from talking to him about my concerns and being confused.

"Great, well want to come on a drive with me?"

"Shouldn't you be in class right now, we still have two periods left in school?"

"Nah, you know me." He brushed it off, making me laugh, he was always skipping classes.

"Not all of us are skippers like you." I joked making him grin.

"C'mon Flo, just this once be a skipper with me."

"No, no, no." I squeezed my eyes shut and laughed, "I will not be a skipper with you." I shook my head.

"Flo, Flo. Look at me." I opened my eyes and blinked. He batted his eyelashes at me, "How could you say no to this face? Could you really do it?"

"Okay, let's go." I finally spoke. He took my hand and almost ran out the door with me, leading me to his car and opening the door for me on my side. "M'lady." He gestured and I hopped in. Once he closed my door he skipped around to his side and got in.

We drove around for a while and found an iHop a good bit away from our neighborhood. We had pancakes and chatted, Eric seemed to generally be in a good mood today. Sometimes he could be reserved and sulky but now, he was happy as ever, smiling goofily, laughing and joking with me. He wasn't worrying about who would see us or what they would think, that's when I liked being around him the most, but I knew it wouldn't last for long. It made my stomach knot at the thought of it. Soon, we would have to go back home and pretend we were strangers again.

Chapter 4

Florence:

The music was pumping loudly from Charlotte's stereo in her bedroom as we both got ready for the party. Saturday had arrived and Charlotte eventually convinced me to go to this party, she could be so persuasive sometimes.

She put half of her long dark hair into a ponytail on the top of her head with a velvet scrunchie and walked over to the stereo to higher up the dance music. Her parents were going to be gone for the whole night so we didn't care if anyone could hear us or not.

"What's with the music?" I raised a brow at her. I didn't mind listening to it but it wasn't her usual style. She always listened to rock or alternative bands from before we were even born.

"It's my getting ready music. You like?" she wiggled her eyebrows and began moving her hips in her acid wash overalls. She always had this grunge nineties look going on and personally I loved it. I wasn't as stylish as

Charlotte, I couldn't pull it off, and I wore what I felt like wearing. I didn't necessarily have a bad fashion sense, but I wouldn't say it was really that good either. I wore a chunky knitted burgundy dress that clung to my hips nicely, some ripped tights and a pair of Nike sneakers. My hair was messy in loose waves that hung just below my shoulders and my makeup was minimal. I had just filled in my brows and coated my long lashes lightly with mascara.

We danced around happily for a minute or two and then began getting ready again. I put on some earrings and bangles and was ready to go. We walked to the party, it only being a few minutes' away and arrived just after ten. The house was already filled with people and music was pumping loudly from inside as we stepped foot on the lawn in front of his house. There were a few people scattered around but it wasn't as busy as the house when we finally stepped in.

I was surprised at the crowds of people. I'd never spoke to this many people before in my life, how did Evan invite so many of them? Charlotte grabbed my hand and began guiding us towards the kitchen to get a drink. Evan, Eric and Mick were there, Eric sitting on the counter telling a story animatedly while the other two watched and listened very carefully. Evan's eyes then wandered to us and he smiled at Charlotte, motioning us to come over. Oh god, I thought, I'd rather not. I walked hesitantly over with her.

"Hey." She called when we were nearly beside them.

"Glad you could make it Charlotte and um...'

"Florence." I tried to smile at him. He brought Charlotte in for a tight hug before letting his gaze fall over her body.

"Well don't forget to grab a drink, there's plenty here." He spoke loudly over the music and motioned to the fridge and the counter lined with spirits. We had already started drinking at Charlotte's house but we weren't drunk yet. "These are my friends Mick," he pointed at Mick who kept a bored expression on his face, "And Eric." He then pointed at Eric, I smiled at him but he didn't smile back.

"Hey." Eric waved unenthusiastically, "Anyway." he said, being kind of dismissive like he wanted to go back to his conversation. Fine then... I thought.

"Let's go Charlotte." I said, picking up two cups and filling them with mixer. I then lead her through the kitchen to the living room where everyone was dancing and the music was the loudest. We took our drink out and poured it in our cups. I was kind of annoyed at Eric, I knew we would have to pretend like we were strangers but he didn't need to be so rude back there. I shouldn't let him get to me but I did.

I drank the whole drink in one, maybe the vodka would help me loosen up a little. We danced for a bit, me continuing to take sups of the vodka straight that I had brought with me every minute or two until it was almost gone.

My mind began to get a little fuzzy and all I wanted to do was just dance to the thumping music that was surrounding me. I felt a bit dizzy and Charlotte noticed this, I was about to take another sip of my drink when she stopped me.

"Whoa slow down Florence, we've only been here an hour. You need to pace yourself." She looked worried.

"You wait here while I grab you some water. Don't drink anymore." I nodded and smiled at her but as soon as she left I drank the last little bit I had left and made my way out to the back garden were there was more music playing. I saw Eric sitting on the stairs with Chloe, a girl from his grade. Their faces were close together and they seemed to be flirting with each other. He never saw me and I quickly walked all the way outside now. There was a lot more people out here than the crowded living room so I decided to stay out for a while.

I moved my body to the beat of the music, trying to get my mind off of Eric, Chloe and the hurt I felt because of it. I knew we weren't an item, I knew he wasn't mine and

I knew we could both be with other people because of this but I just didn't expect to be so upset by it.

I honestly didn't know why I was doing this but the thought never stopped me at the time I moved into the middle of the crowd and danced. I was usually a little shy and just so quiet in crowds of people but right now, I could care less as I dancing surrounded by everyone. A pair of hands rested on my waist as someone began to dance with me. We were all so close together and when I turned around I was surprised to see Kane, a jock from my year grinning at me and dancing.

"You can really move Florence." He said as we both got more into it. How does he know my name? I thought, he's never even spoke to me before, no one knows my name.

"I Wish I could say the same about you." I flirted back and winked at him. We moved closer to each other, our bodies touching slightly when we danced. I turned around with my back to him and swayed my hips with the music. His hands had now lowered from my waist to my hips. He whispered in my ear and kissed my neck. I didn't really care what I was doing, if Eric could do whatever he liked, so could I. We were moving together, even closer than before if that was possible when a hand grabbed mine and dragged me away from him. I looked up to see a very pissed off Eric staring back between me and Kane.

"Get your hands off of her." He growled.

"Hey man, we were in the middle of something." Kane replied, starting to get annoyed now too.

"Well not anymore." He said before leading me farther away from Kane. I didn't attempt to go back because of the look Eric had given me. We were around the side of the house now, it was empty and dark.

"What the hell were you doing back there?" he was really angry now.

"What did it look like? I was dancing." I tried not to slur my words.

"You know what I mean." He glared at me. I rolled my eyes and turned around, beginning to make my way back to the garden.

"Where are you going?" he took my arm again. I turned around and looked at him, he seemed more concerned than angry now.

"I'm going back to dance with Kane, because Kane isn't afraid to talk to me in public." I crossed my arms. I knew that was I was probably being a bitch right now but I didn't care. His eyes lost their hardness at my words and he didn't speak for what felt like minutes.

"Whatever Flo. Why don't you just go back to Kane then?" Didn't he just stop me from going back to Kane?

He sounded really hurt but at that point in time, I didn't care, I was sick of caring.

"Why don't you just go back to Chloe?" I shot back. It was like the penny had finally dropped in his mind.

"What's that supposed to mean?" he narrowed his eyes but he knew what I meant.

"I saw you two on the stairs."

"Don't be so jealous Flo."

"Me? Jealous?!" I threw my hands up in the air. "You have to be kidding me, I wouldn't waste my time. I'm not the one who walked in and stopped what was happening now was I?" I squinted at him. We never fought before, this was so weird. Was I jealous? No, I couldn't be. I was just angry at myself for being so stupid and never thinking about him being with other girls because I had never even thought of anyone else since we started this not-a-relationship relationship with him. He hadn't got anything else to say because he knew I was right, so I started walking away again.

"Look I'm sorry, I just- I don't know. I just..."

"You just what?" I turned around and looked at him.

"Nothing, I shouldn't have gotten jealous." He admitted.

"Exactly, because we aren't a couple, we are both allowed to do whatever we want."

"Yes, I know." It looked like the words were painful coming out of his mouth but they shouldn't be, I wasn't the one that was so keen on not having a relationship. "Just because I don't want to go out with you doesn't mean I don't care about you Flo." He looked so vulnerable standing in front of me now. I didn't know what to say, my eyes widened slightly at his words. Was he drunk? He didn't seem drunk to me. He had moved closer, ducking down so his face was neared to mine and he was looking me straight in the eye. He gulped before sayings "Please, just don't go back there to him. Stay with me." I still couldn't find the words to speak and my temper had calmed down. All I could do was nod slightly at him before he took my hand and led me inside again. I was trying my best not to fall because I felt dizzier than ever now. Soon enough, Eric noticed this.

"Are you okay?" he looked at me quizzically; there was a hint of humor in his voice as he tried to hide a smile.

"Perfect." I grinned at him.

"You're drunk." He chuckled. "C'mon, let's get you a glass of water." We ended up in the kitchen. I wondered where Charlotte was I hadn't seen her in a while now, maybe she was with Evan. Eric handed me the glass of water and I threw it over my shoulder, pretending to drink it , at first he laughed. But it was all over the floor and I couldn't control my giggling now, Eric got some paper towels to clean it up and while he was on the ground I grabbed a bottle of something from the counter and ran.

I heard Eric call after me but he was too late, I was mixed into the crowd. I was dancing and twirling around, swigging from the bottle and wincing every time at the taste, I made my way around the large house. It's so much bigger than my house, it's decorated nicely too. It was as big as Eric's house, maybe Evan's mom and dad were fancy lawyers too. Or maybe not. I made my way up the stairs, it was empty up here. God the carpet looks so soft, I bent down and touched the white carpet, it was even softer than I imagined. Maybe Evan won't mind if I just lie on it for a while, I thought. And without even noticing, I drifted off to sleep.

Chapter 5

Eric:

I unlocked my front door quietly and tip-toed in. After five minutes of convincing Florence to come upstairs with me, she finally agreed. Although she was a little louder than I would've liked, she got into my room in one piece. She closed the door to my room loudly and kicked her shoes off, both flying to opposite sides of the room. One smacked against my wall making a loud thumping noise and the other hit my desk, making my lamp fall off and clatter to the ground. She kept giggling and saying "Shh." Like I was the one making all of the noise.

I helped her half-asleep-half-drunken self out of her dress and tights and into one of my t-shirts before placing her carefully on one side of my bed. I pulled the covers over her but she kicked them off again when I went to get her a glass of water. I placed the glass on the bed side table and knelt down, her back was to me but she turned around and looked at me once I tipped her to get her attention.

"Flo, I need you to listen to me okay?" I talked to her like you would talk to a four year old child and tried to get her attention but she was too busy playing with my hair. I put my hands on hers and stopped her. "You need to go to bed now, so put the covers over you and try to go asleep." She nodded; her round eyes looked tired but cute. I then got myself ready to go asleep and hopped into bed beside her, holding her in my arms.

She eventually drifted off to sleep and was the quietest I'd seen her all night. I let out a sigh of relief. She made some things difficult tonight but she was definitely worth all of the trouble. I had to convince her friend to let her go home with me, well I didn't tell her we would end up in my house because she thought I barely knew her, I knew she didn't completely believe that though.

She must've known something was up between us two because she eventually let me take her home. I told them she lived around the corner from me and I would make sure she got home safe. She agreed that Florence probably needed to go home rather than stay at the party and sleep at her house but she was very hesitant to let me go with her.

She was extremely worried at first and offered to bring her home herself but Florence mumbled something in her drunken state and after that, I could almost see the penny drop in her friends mind.

"Are we going to your house again Eric?" Florence mumbled loudly to me. "I love your house." She giggled. I looked up and Charlotte was staring between both me and Florence quizzically but she never said anything to us. I was so glad. It took us over half an hour to get home, I walked that route on other days in about ten minutes but it was longer because I had to almost carry her home.

She snuggled up closer to me now and nuzzled her head against my neck and bare shoulders. She looked so peaceful when she was sleeping. I held her closer and kissed her forehead. She was just so perfect to me. I really liked her, ever since that day she walked by me out in the corridor in school last year, she just caught my eye. I thought she was new, I had never really noticed her before that but as soon as I seen her, all I done was notice her.

She wasn't like any of the other girls I used to hook up with, not at all. The thought scared me a little because I knew with her it was very different. I actually began to see myself caring about her the more we spent time together. The only thing that was stopping me from admitting to myself or Florence or anyone else that I needed her and that she meant so much to me was keeping what we had a secret.

I think I believed if I pretended that most of the time we were barely even acquaintances, then I could make myself believe that all of it wasn't real. Because even though one half of me wanted her, the other was anxious about it all. I don't need a relationship, it's better for the both of us to stay the way we are now, but I knew there was only so many times I could push her away before she would eventually leave me alone for good, and that was the exact opposite of what I really needed or wanted.I was starting to slip up more and more over the past few weeks, I was beginning to let my guard down and I wasn't being as strict with myself, I was beginning to realize I actually cared about her. An example was right now, god, we didn't even do it and she was still staying in my bed with me.

I knew that a relationship was definitely what I didn't need, that didn't mean I didn't want it either did it? I knew I wouldn't be able to see her with another person. I was the jealous type, but only when I really cared. I acted a bit harshly tonight when I see her with Kane but I couldn't stop myself. It was unfair of me, considering I had been talking to and flirting with other people at the party too. I needed Mick and my other friends to not get too suspicious. Chloe was a friend, even if I knew she was interested, and without trying to be mean, she was nothing compared to Florence but then again who was?

I had to make a decision sooner rather than later, would I go back to being my guarded self with Florence or would I start show how much more I wanted with her?

Chapter 6

Florence:

The sun light streamed in from the window in the room and woke me up. As soon as I opened my eyes, I closed them again, it was way too bright for me to handle right now. I lifted my head up and then suddenly I felt the thumping in my head. I winced in pain and sunk my head back onto Eric's chest. Wait, Eric? I thought and quickly shot my head back up. I jolted out of bed, ignoring my headache and the fact that I might wake him up and quickly got dressed. I left his room and darted down the stairs.

A million thoughts raced through my mind. Where's Charlotte? Does she know I stayed with Eric? What did I do last night? And how did I get here? Little snippets of the party that I could remember replayed in my mind. I remembered seeing Eric and Chloe on the stairs and I remember dancing with Kane. Oh god, what else happened after I fell asleep on the floor in one of Evan's bedrooms? I have never felt more embarrassed than I do right now.

And now, here I was again, making my way back home from Eric's house early enough that no one would see me. I was beginning to get tired of all of this. I didn't want to admit to myself that last night, maybe I was a little jealous because then that would mean I cared when I shouldn't.

When we began this whole thing, the one thing I knew I couldn't do was care because it wouldn't be given back to me in return. In the beginning, I was a lot more naïve than I am now, I was kind of upset that Eric didn't want anything to do with me unless it was just the two of us but I soon snapped out of it. I knew if I wanted a relationship, I should find someone else. But I didn't want anyone else and I still don't.

I groaned at my confusing thoughts as I turned the key in my door and snuck in, closing the door very gently as to not wake my dad. Once I made my way to my room, I got under the covers of my bed and drifted off to sleep but woke up a few hours later to the sound of my phone ringing on my bedside table. It took me a while to get the motivation to move just a little to pick it up and answer.

"Hello." I groaned.

"Oh Florence, thank god you're alright! I've been so worried about you ever since you left with Eric." She sounded so relieved.

"Yeah, I'm fine now."

"So what did your dad say when you got in last night?" she sounded intrigued.

"Um, yeah he was kind of annoyed." I lied. So Eric told her he was bringing me home. Of course he did, he doesn't want anyone to know about you, I thought.

"I'm so sorry I didn't go home with you Florence, I understand if you're annoyed at me. Seriously."

"It's okay-"

"Florence!" I heard my dad calling me from downstairs.

"Sorry Charlotte, I have to go but I'll talk to you later." I said before hanging up and quickly exiting my bedroom and making my way to the kitchen were my dad was.

"Hey dad." I said groggily.

"You okay kiddo?" he asked, he seemed very spritely today.

"Yeah, just have a bit of a- headache." I replied.

"There's aspirin in the cupboard above the sink." He did this thing where he pretended that I didn't consume alcohol the night before, even when he knew I did which was rarely ever.

"Thanks." I reached up and got the box of pills.

"So how was the party last night? I heard you getting in very early from Charlotte's." he looked up from his paper at me.

"Yeah, I just felt like sleeping in my own bed." I said before swallowing the tablets with glass of water.

"Hey, you want to come help out in the shop today? We just got a big delivery in and I could really use the extra pair of hands." I smiled at him, spending some time with him would be good so I agreed and ran upstairs to take a shower.

The pills kicked in a few minutes later and along with the greasy bacon and eggs my dad made me, I felt good as new. We drove in my dad's car to the shop and when we got in, I noticed a tall figure standing at the back of the shop, stocking up shelves. He had short brown hair and was wearing some sort of dark blue work apron.

"Hiya Jake, how's it going?" My dad asked.

"Not too bad sir." He said but didn't turn around yet, he was in the middle of sorting something. "How are you doing?" he asked and turned around when he was finished. He stood frozen in his spot for a second. I finally caught a glimpse of his face, his dark brows raised a little in surprise and his warm green eyes turned up at the end when he smiled at me. God, he was hot, I thought.

"Jake, this is my daughter Florence. Florence, this is Jake."

"Hi." His voice was deep.

"Hi." I said shyly. Sure, when it came to friends I was definitely not shy, but with strangers I became so shy and quiet, especially with cute kind.

"So I have finally met the famous Florence. Your dad never stops talking about you." He held his big hand out to shake mine. I laughed a little and shook it.

"Right, let's get to work you two." My dad rubbed his hands together and we all began getting to work.

Lunch rolled around quick enough and both Jake and I went to get ourselves and my dad lunch in the deli down the street in town. As we entered, my phone buzzed and I took it out of my pocket.

Eric: Hey, how are you after last night? Want to grab something to eat in a while?:)

As soon as I seen his name, I remembered seeing him and Chloe again. I had completely forgotten about him after I left early this morning. Why was he with Chloe? Why was I jealous? Did he explain anything to me? Not that he needed to, I mean I shouldn't care should I? God this was confusing me now more than it ever did. I think I was beginning to get fed up with it all, or was it because I as starting to care a little more than I should. Why all the questions Florence?! Calm down.

"Hey, you okay?" Jake put his hand on my shoulder, stopping my thoughts from running even farther away with themselves.

"Yeah, yeah I'm fine. Let's get lunch." I smiled at him and told Eric that I couldn't today.

We both sat down to eat and got my dad's lunch to go. My first impression of Jake was that he was a really nice guy; he was funny too and never stopped talking the whole time. I was a lot more comfortable with him after our chat over lunch than I was when I first saw him.

We headed back to the shop to give my dad his lunch and get back to work. Eric texted me back but I was pre-occupied so I didn't check my phone until Jake drove me home. My dad stayed later at the shop and told us to go ahead. His car was nice enough, better than my wore out Toyota, I couldn't complain though, at least I had a car.

Eric: Maybe another time then?:(

I didn't reply. Why did he suddenly want to see me? He wants to see me and talk to me one day but the next he ignores me completely and doesn't even look in my direction, it was all confusing but as we pulled up to my house I decided that maybe I needed to pull back a bit from this thing Eric and I had. I wasn't ready to face my feelings yet. I was lying to myself and keeping my own secrets because if I ever told Eric, I knew he would most likely run and leave me high and dry. I had finally made up my mind: I was a wimp, I was shying away from telling Eric how I felt about a lot of things but instead of facing the problem, I wouldn't be as hopeful that we would become normal with each other. This was our normal, as much as I was beginning to see the light and noticing how much I really hated it or not. I would somewhat remove myself from the situation and see what it was like without him again. I needed it, his mixed signals and guardedness were a little too much for me to handle right now.

Chapter 7

Eric:

"What are you doing?" I pushed Michael, a guy I knew from the football team, away from another figure that was now on the ground of the school halls.

"None of your business man. Stay out of it." Michael and his friends laughed. They had clearly been picking on the person on the ground. He looked up, he looked kind of shocked. That was when I noticed it was one of Flo's friends. I knew his face from around school when I saw him with her.

"What's funny?" I moved closer to one of the other guys there how and he instantly stopped laughing, gulping loudly. I moved away and turned to Michael and the rest of his friends.

"Stay away from him." I said angrily, sure I could have a joke and a laugh but bullying was just something I hated. My words seemed to have scared them a bit; the four boys looked at me with wide eyes. "What the hell are you all still doing here?" I grabbed Michael by his collar and moved my face closer to his. He shrugged out of my grip and the group scurried off.

"You okay man?" I asked, looking down at Kevin and holding my hand out, offering to help him up. He looked at my hand then at me, hesitantly taking my offer and getting up from the ground.

"Yeah I'm fine." He said quietly, I didn't know much about him but hearing Flo talk about him, he sounded like a loud, overly happy kind of guy. Whenever I seen him with her, he doesn't stop talking. "Thanks." He said before we walked away quickly.

Soon enough, it was lunch time. Mick and I walked into the cafeteria and got lunch. We sat with Evan and the rest of our friends. Evan was texting on his phone, a little pre-occupied. He kept on grinning and laughing at his screen until we finally asked what he was doing even though we didn't need to. It was obvious he was talking to that girl Charlotte from the party last weekend. She was Flo's friend too, the one I had to convince it was okay to let me take her home when she was majorly wasted.

My mind went back to that night and how we finally got home. How she cuddled into me while I lay awake, fighting with my thoughts. She could be so comforting sometimes even when she wasn't even trying. That night was rough. After hours of lying awake, worrying about what we had between us and what was going on in my head about her, was I finally starting to like her more than I liked anyone else I had a thing with? I finally drifted off into a restless sleep and woke up to find she was gone. At the beginning of all of this, sure, I didn't want her to stay the entire night but recently it sounded like a much better idea. It was ironic how now, when I wanted her to stay she never felt like it. Sometimes, it was nice waking up and seeing her.

We hadn't spoken properly since though, I texted her the following day asking her did she want to go out but she declined the offer. Can you imagine? Half of the school wanted that opportunity and she just turned me down. But she never saw me like that; I wasn't someone she pined over childishly, that's one of the things that drew me to her at the start. She was different.

I scanned the vast amount of tables in the cafeteria, searching for her face. My eyes landed on her, she was talking animatedly and pointing at her phone, showing her friends something. Her short brown hair was wavy and messy, like it always was and it bounced as she threw her head back with laughter. I wished I sat closer so I could hear her but what felt like a million conversations going on at the one time drowned out her warm chuckles and sweet voice. I wished everyone would just shut up so I could hear her talk.

She was sitting with her three friends, who were listening and laughing along with her. Kevin was there, he seemed to be back to his usual self, along with Charlotte who would look at her phone every so often to reply to Evan and some other girl who was petite and had a short pastel pink bob. Flo never looked over at me once, she was too busy. She seemed like that a lot lately, brushing off my attempts to see her. Was something wrong? This was second time she had done this and recently it felt like we hadn't been talking properly or communicating that much at all. I need to talk to her, soon.

"Hey, Eric." Mick shook my shoulder. "What are you looking at?" he looked in the direction I had been looking and realized I had been staring at Florence for the past few minutes. "Oh-h-h, I see." He winked at me and the rest of the guys laughed.

"What's he looking at Mick?" One of them asked.

"That girl, what's-her-face. I can't remember her name. Hey Eric, is she new or something?" I didn't say anything. "She got wasted at Evan's party last weekend, passed out on his floor, do you remember her?" Mick replied to the group.

"Yeah, she's kind of hot." One of them said which made me immediately glare at him.

"She's been going here since freshman year, she's not new at all." I told Mick between gritted teeth.

"You sound very protective there bro, especially towards a person you've only talked to once." Mick squinted at me, challenging me. Whoa, was I getting protective? No, maybe a little defensive but that was just because I knew her and they didn't right?

"Whatever." I grumbled and continued eating my food. Mick was really pissing me off.

I looked up at Florence again when no one was watching. She was smiling and then our eyes met, her grin disappeared and turned into a frown before she quickly looked away again. What was her problem? Did I do something to annoy her? She was confusing me, she never usually got like this. We definitely needed to talk.

Chapter 8

Florence:

I looked over and found Eric's blue eyes staring at me. I frowned and looked away, I hadn't spoken to him in a while now, I kind of missed him but I finally made up my mind. It was a hard decision to make and even harder hiding how I felt around everyone because I couldn't open up and tell them what was going on in my mind. I began talking again and trying to eat my food but I didn't feel hungry anymore. I got up and left the table, telling Kevin, Charlotte and Emma I needed to go to the bathroom.

As soon as I exited the cafeteria, I made my way towards the bathrooms. I heard the doors of the cafeteria opening and closing again and then footsteps coming towards me.

"Flo." I heard Eric call, still a good bit behind me. I walked faster. "Flo!" He called, even louder now. Please, anybody but him, I thought. I knew it would be unfair to not give him an explanation but I was chicken, especially when it came to things like this with Eric. He had caught up with me now and stopped me in my tracks, standing in front of me. I looked up at him with tired eyes, I really wasn't in the mood right now. "What's wrong with you?" he asked, sounding a little concerned.

"Nothing." I brushed him off and tried to walk away but he stopped me again.

"Why are you avoiding me?" he looked at me with pain in his eyes. I shrugged. "God damn it Florence answer me!" his voice dripped with frustration. I avoided his eyes for a moment, deciding whether to just be honest with him or not. "Flor-"

"I'm tired of this okay?" I was getting angry now too. I looked him in the eye, his expression dropped. Was it panic maybe? No it couldn't be. "I'm tired of keeping things from everyone and acting like I don't even know you when other people are around."

"You know I don't want a relationship Florence."

"And neither do I, that's not what I'm getting at." I said through gritted teeth. Was he trying to make me out to needy? I wasn't needy, I didn't want to go out with him either. I just wanted to be able not hide things from my friends, I wanted to be able to look for advice and I wanted to just hang out with him whenever we wanted without making sure no one we knew was around. It was seriously getting on my nerves the more I thought about it. "We should just quit while we're ahead." I finally said. He looked really angry now.

"Why? What's wrong with this? Do you want to tell everyone about us or something?" he demanded, I knew he was getting agitated now.

"I never said I wanted to tell everyone. I just-"

"Good, because there's nothing to tell. There's nothing between us Florence and there never will be, you were just someone I fooled around with every once in a while." His words were like venom, burning through my heart. Tears pricked my eyes but I refused to cry in front of him. I was shocked at how much his words hurt but I didn't want to stand there any longer and show him how much he affected me.

"Fuck you." I spat before brushing past him and storming off towards the bathrooms. God I was so angry and just so heartbroken at the same time. You were just someone I fooled around with every once in a while, his words rang in my ears again. Why was I so stupid? I knew that was what this meant to him all along, why did I try to pretend it wasn't? I felt so horrible and hurt and I just didn't want to think about it anymore. I never imagined I would allow myself to feel like this over Eric. I knew all along what I was getting myself into.

I didn't feel like going back to lunch or to any classes I had after it so I walked out of school and went straight to the nearest McDonalds for comfort food and then on a very long drive to clear my head. I had all of my windows open as I flew down empty roads, not caring where they took me. I had the radio turned up full blast and all I done for a good three hours was listened and ate and cried every now and then.

Why was I getting so upset? You know why Florence, I thought. You really did a good job at pretending you didn't care about Eric, but you know you really do, even if he doesn't care about you too. But then I remembered what he said that night at the party, just because I don't want to go out with you doesn't mean I don't care about you, that was such a lie! It made another tear slip down my cheek. Why was I still crying? Snap out of it Florence!

My thoughts were just one big blur, I was confused as hell. I began to make my way to the park a few minutes away from where I lived. I parked and got out of the car, making my way to the more reserved part beside the lake. There were no benches so I sat down on the grass, watching the ducks waddle and swim around. Because it was mid-February, it didn't get dark as early anymore and the sun was just beginning to set, making the sky a beautiful orange-blue color. I sat there for a while, still feeling slightly down but not as bad as before. Eric wasn't worth it.

Just then, I heard barking and someone shouting.

"Skip! Come back here now!" The owner demanded. I turned around but it was too late to get up now. The dog was running towards in my direction and jumped on me, licking my face. I squirmed and opened my eyes when it stopped to see a huge German Shepard breathing heavily and smiling at me, his tongue hanging out of his mouth as he did so.

"Skip!" The voice sounded familiar and like it was getting closer now. I laughed at the dog's expression as it tilted its head to the side, staring back at me. "Oh my god, I'm so sorry- Florence?" the person stood by my side. I looked from the brown work-shoes beside my face all the way up to the person's face.

"Hey." He said sheepishly, he looked embarrassed now.

"Hey."

Chapter 9

Florence:

"Hey." I said, my voice shook a little. I pushed Skip gently off of me and sat up, crossing my legs. Skip sat beside me and I patted his head.

"Are you alright?" Jake bent down to my level now and I avoided eye contact with him. He looked at my face for a second and then furrowed his brows but didn't say anything else.

"Yeah I'm fine, I'm just thinking you know?" I asked him.

"Yeah. Hey I know I probably shouldn't ask you this because it's none of my business or anything but have you been crying?"

"No." I lied. I knew my swollen eyes would give me away. He sat down beside me and looked at me with concern but I think he knew I didn't want to talk about it. For now, I was over it, I was all cried out. We both sat there and looked out onto the lake in comfortable silence. Jake began talking after a while, he and Skip really cheered me up.

"You want to go grab something to eat?" he asked. I looked at him for a moment, deciding whether to go or not. It had been some time since I binged out on twenty chicken nuggets, a cheeseburger and a large strawberry milkshake. I was getting a little hungry now.

"Sure." I smiled at him.

"Okay then, I just need to drop Skip home and then we can go." He said as we both got up.

"I drove here so where will I meet you when you're done?"

"Oh no it's fine. I'll drive, we can come pick your car up on the way home when we're finished if you like?" that did sound like a better idea.

"Yeah, alright let's go." I nodded and we began walking to Jake's car, Skip tagging along by my side. When we got in he decided he would rather sit on my lap, crushing me because he was so heavy. He just turned his head a few times to look at me, I couldn't help but laugh and Jake began to as well.

"He really likes you." He said when we were on his way to his house.

"You think?" I joked as I patted Skip on the head.

"I don't blame him, what's not to like about you." He said, causing me to look up at him. He was unaffected, looking straight at the road as he drove. I blushed slightly but he couldn't see me.We reached Jake's house soon enough and when Jake opened my door, Skip hopped out.

"You want to come in?" he asked me.

"Um, no it's fine really. I don't mind waiting here."

"C'mon. My mom doesn't bite. I swear." He winked and joked. I laughed at him and decided to go in.

"We won't be long anyway. I just need to drop Skip in." We walked up to his door and he turned the key in the lock, signalling for me to go first.

"Mom! I'm home." He called. As soon as we entered, the smell of cooking hit me. I followed him into the kitchen where we met his mother, standing at a stove stirring a pot and his dad sitting down at the counter. His mother was short with dark hair hanging down her back. Jake walked past her to let Skip out into the back garden and you could really see how tall he was now.

"And who's this?" His father asked and smiled at me. He was a tall man with green eyes and dark hair like Jake.

"This is Florence, I work for her dad down at the store." Put his arm around me and I welcomed his warmth. He smelled good.

"Oh hello, I didn't see you there!" his mom turned around and grinned at me.

"How are you dear?"

"I'm fine thank you." I smiled shyly at her.

"We were about to go out and get something to eat, I'll be back in a while."

"Oh a date is it? I hope he's treating you right dear." She finally said, causing my cheeks to burn and my face flush a dark red color.

"Mom!" Jake said in embarrassment.

"C'mon Florence, we should go." He guided me out the door.

"It was nice meeting you Florence." His mom and dad waved at me as we left the kitchen.

"Nice meeting you too." I called back, they were really so friendly but I was embarrassed now.

"I'm sorry about them." he laughed a little. "Anyways, let's get going."We were both not in the mood for anything fancy so we went this quiet diner in town. There weren't many people there so we didn't have to wait for a table. After we ordered our food and the waitress took the menu's from us, we began chatting.

"So where do you go to school then Florence?" he looked at me with his green eyes, they were warm and somehow inviting.

"Just to the high school down the road. And you?"

"Oh I don't go to high school anymore, thank god. I just did my first year at Farebrooke University." He smiled at me.

"But you still live around here?" I asked.

"Yeah, I tried living on campus but I'd rather get up the extra few minutes early and drive. I work here and I've always lived here so I don't want to leave just yet. I'm a bit of a home bird you know?"

"Yeah, I know." I smiled back at him. He had dimples on both cheeks that you could only see when he smiled, it was cute. Eric didn't have dimples, okay Florence shut up you are with Jake now. Not Eric. I thought to myself. We continued to talk over dinner, he was an English major and he really loved college. He wanted to travel too, and journalism was something that appealed to him so hopefully he would get a career in it in years to come. He had two older sisters who lived away from home and his family were very close.

Before we knew it, it was almost ten and was dark outside. We got the bill and Jake decided that he would not let me pay. After five minutes of arguing with him, he slapped the money down on the table and I was forced to reluctantly accepted that I would not be paying.

Jake dropped me to my car and told me he would text me to make sure I got home alright. We had exchanged numbers a few days ago when he dropped me home from my dad's store. I drove home and after telling my nosey dad that I was with Jake, I went upstairs to my room to get ready for bed. I got changed into a baggy t-shirt and shorts and then curled up under the covers in bed.

My phone buzzed on my bedside table and when I reached over and looked at it, it was a message from Jake.

Jake: Hope you got home okay, text me back so I know you weren't kidnapped or something:/:)

I laughed and replied that I really was fine, I got home a while ago and I really needed to get some sleep or I wouldn't be able to get up tomorrow for school. As I set my phone back down on the table beside me, I began to think about everything that happened today. Jake was a really nice guy and he got my mind off of a lot of things without me even having to tell him about Eric. As soon as his name entered my thoughts, I couldn't get it to leave. I fell asleep with his bright blue eyes in my mind.

Chapter 10

Eric:

I missed her. I really fucking missed her. I so badly wanted to just give her a call or a text but as soon as I picked up my phone, I would remember the last time we had spoken and all if the stupid things I had said to her. I wanted to talk to her and just make sure she was okay but I knew if she wasn't it would be my fault.I needed time to think about our situation and I was trying to make up my mind. I guess my mouth decided for me before my brain could.

The more I thought about it, the more I became just so frustrated at myself for what I had done. And the more I thought about that, the more I wished I had picked the other option. I had just gotten so annoyed so quickly and I spoke too soon.I didn't want to be pushed into a relationship with her when I didn't need one. I told myself so many times before that it would just be better without one and that they were a waste of time. I knew now, looking back on what she was saying that maybe that wasn't what she meant when she said she was tired of hiding things. I knew she didn't like keeping secrets. I understood because sometimes I felt like that too but keeping us simply between us meant that I didn't have to face my feelings.

I didn't mean what I said to her, I didn't mean any of it. I told her how she was just like everyone else which was the exact opposite of what I felt. She was so different. She looked so hurt by my words, when she walked off all I wanted to do was call her back and tell her I was sorry but I just stood there, trying to figure out why I done what I done.

Every day I seemed to see her more often than I usually would before our argument. And when I passed her in the halls she wouldn't even glance at me, I examined her face every time I passed her. She had tired eyes and her hair was messier than usual. When she talked to her friends she would smile but it wouldn't reach her eyes.

It had been three weeks now since we had spoken. I was still beating myself up and feeling pitiful and my friends noticed. The more time I spent not talking to Flo, the more I thought about her. It got to the point where I thought of little else. Something was stopping me from just apologizing to her, I never apologize to anyone but this time was different. I knew I had to, I wanted to.

"Hey you okay man?" I heard Evan call from beside me. We were getting at practice but my mind was somewhere else completely.

"Yeah." I nodded but I knew I didn't sound very convincing.

"You sure? You seem a bit tied up lately. You don't look like you're enjoying yourself at all. C'mon, this is football, you're favorite thing to do remember?" he patted my on the shoulder and tried to give an encouraging speech but I just was not in the mood.

"I just need to sort some things out. Will you tell coach I had to leave early?" I asked him.

"Sure, but you know he'll have a fit."

"Just tell him my dog died."

"But you don't have a dog?" He laughed.

"Just tell him." I said before I ran back into the locker rooms and grabbed my duffel bag and the rest of my things. I needed to go on a run; it always helped to clear my head.

When I got home my mom greeted me from the kitchen. She was probably drinking coffee and surrounded by a tonne of paperwork on the kitchen table like she usually was: Always working hard. I said hey and climbed up the stairs, heading for my bedroom to get into my running gear.

It was starting to get dark by now, I didn't know how long I had been running but I began making my back to my house. I turned the corner onto Florence's street and continued to jog until I seen a car pull up at her driveway down the street. I slowed down slightly when I heard her laughter and the car door opened.She went around to the driver's side of the car and leaned her elbows on the opened window. Who was in the car? Who was she talking to? I thought. I was getting closer now.

"Thanks so much for the ride Jake- No I'll be fine on my own, my dad should be home in a couple of hours anyway- see you." She smiled and then walked back up onto the pavement as the car drove off. Who was this Jake guy? She walked up her driveway and my body came to a halt in front of her house. I didn't know what I was doing, my mind was telling me to keep going but my legs thought otherwise. She's going to think you're some kind of stalker dumb ass, don't just stand there.

But it was too late to run off now because she was already turned around, looking at me with that drained expression on her face. She ruffled her messy hair with her hands, looking uncomfortable. We didn't say a word, just looked at each other in silence for a moment or two.

"What do you want Eric?" I could hear the discomfort in her voice as her droopy eyes showed only a sadness. I tried to think of an answer to her question but I couldn't.

I opened and closed my mouth a few times but no words were coming out. What was I doing here?

Chapter 11

Florence:

I stood there in shock, why was he even here?

"What do you want Eric?" I asked, trying to hold back any emotion in my voice but I knew I had failed. Tears began to prick my eyes as I took in his appearance. I hadn't really looked at him in weeks. There was something different about him, he appeared tired and worn out but why? He began walking closer to me now but I took a step back until I hit my front door.

"I miss you.' He finally spoke. It looked like it took him a lot to say it but I was trying to figure out whether he was being genuine or not. I went to speak but closed my mouth again. I had so much and so little to say it him, I just didn't know how to begin. To tell him I didn't miss him would be a complete lie, I couldn't stop thinking about him and everything that has happened with the two of us in the past few months. But it was a tricky situation, what we had between us.

Just because I missed him didn't mean I would just fall to his feet because the feeling was mutual. I missed talking to him, I missed hanging out with him, I even missed just seeing him for a second when we passed by each other on the corridors because I had to force myself to stop looking. His words hurt more than I ever thought they would and when that happened, I just knew I wasn't doing the right thing but I didn't care anymore.

"I-"

"And I'm sorry about what I said a while ago."

"But-"

"And I know that you might not want to talk to me again because what I said was horrible Flo. It was just plain mean and I didn't even know what I was doing. It's okay if you never talk to me ever again, well actually it wouldn't' be because I don't want that- "he was rambling on and all I could do was listen intently at what he was saying, or at least, trying to say. "Look, I just, I- I don't know Flo." He sounded frustrated now, combing his hands through his golden blonde hair. "I just really fucking miss you and what I said? Well it's not true, you mean something to me. You aren't like anyone else and that's what I like about you. I care about you Flo, more than you can ever think."

He finally looked at me after taking a breath he had been holding while he was talking. He had apologetic eyes but I just didn't know what to say. What was I supposed to say? I had never been in this situation before, we never had fights. We just stared at each other for a moment but he was getting closer to me now.

"I-I missed you too." I finally said as a tear rolled down my cheek. No need to cry Flo, get a hold of yourself, I thought. He moved in front of me and cupped my cheek, whipping the tear with his thumbs.

"Don't cry, please. I didn't mean to make you cry. I'm sorry."Our faces were centimeters apart, our eyes were locked on each other and he had both his hands on either side of my face. He kissed me gently at first, I didn't even think about pulling away. I missed his lips. He deepened the kiss and one of my hands flew up to tangle between his hair while the other unlocked the door.

We both walked in, me walking backwards to the living room. He stopped for a second to catch his breath and kicked the door closed before following me to the sofa. We were both on the couch now; he pulled his shirt over his head, exposing his toned chest. His hands reached behind my back and pulled me closer as he traced kisses down my neck. His lips met mine again, this time more urgently as he unbuttoned my shirt and took it off.

I didn't stop and think about what I was doing, or how I told myself before that I should stay away from him. The thought wouldn't have stopped me at this point anyway. I wanted him now; it was too late to stop.

After that night I saw a lot of Eric, but things were still mostly the same. We never talked when people were around and only stole the occasional glance at each other, like right now in the cafeteria. I smiled at him and he grinned widely back at me. Kevin and Emma were chatting beside me, what else do they do? I thought. Charlotte hadn't turned up for any classes today which was unusual for her.

"Hey, where's Charlotte?" Kevin asked as if reading my thoughts.

"Not sure," I shrugged my shoulders, "She usually tells one of us where she is when she doesn't come to school. Do you know where she is?" I looked at Emma now.

"I don't know either, maybe she's sick." She frowned at me. The weather had gotten warmer now. and that meant Emma would become more colorful if it was even possible. She was wearing a bright yellow sundress with big circle shades on her head holding her pastel purple hair back.

"How's her and lover boy getting on anyway? We haven't heard much about him in a while." Kevin popped a fry into his mouth and looked at me.

"They're doing good actually, I think so anyway." Charlotte and Evan had been dating now for the past few weeks and we could all really tell how much she liked him, he liked her too. They always went out on dates and texted each other whenever they weren't in each others company, it was kind of cute actually. Evan was really sweet to her, I knew this because of the stories she told me about him.

"Well good for her, she deserves someone who's actually nice to, unlike that asshole she dated a while ago."

'That asshole's name was James, but we never spoke about him when Charlotte was around, we never spoke a lot about him when she wasn't around either actually. But James was, just like we had said, a complete asshole to Charlotte; he never treated her well and had little respect for her. Charlotte just didn't realize any of this for a long while after they started dating. She eventually broke off the relationship when he got too much for her to handle. We were just glad she finally listened to us all, but things were going good for her and Evan and we were all so happy for her now.

"Yeah, I know right." I said and picked up my burger to take a bite out of it. We continued our conversation about where Charlotte might be, starting to make a game out of it.

"Maybe she's out saving the world."

"Maybe she's out fighting off bear's with her bare hands."

"Or mountain climbing, she'd love that." Kevin snorted sarcastically. He knew she wasn't much of an outdoors person. At that moment I looked over at Eric's table and seen Evan sitting at the other end, I got an idea.

"Hey, you know what? We could ask Eric, I'm sure he would have some idea."

"Good idea but I'm not asking, you can." Emma demanded.

"We need to go soon anyway, you two promised me you would come help me with my project in the library. Don't pull out on me now bitches." She squinted her eyes in mock disgust. Kevin rolled his eyes.

"I don't want to help you with your dumb project Emma, I'm not the one who left it last minute girl." "Kevin." I warned him. "We promised."

"Okay, okay. Let's go." He grabbed his bag and stood up.

"Go. Go. Go." Emma grabbed my hand as the three of us made our way to the door of the cafeteria and stopped at Eric's table.

"Hey Evan." I spoke up and he looked at me and smiled.

"Yeah, what's up?" he asked in a friendly tone.

"Have you been talking to Charlotte? She didn't turn up to school today."

"Oh yeah, I think she's just sick or something."

"Oh, alright. Thanks anyway Evan."

"Hey Florence." I heard Mick, who was sitting beside Eric call from down the other end of the table. I looked at him in surprise for a second; he was grinning like an idiot and waving at me. I looked between both him and Eric,who was giving him a seething look.

"How's it going?"

"Hello. Em, I'm fine thanks." I waved at him in bewilderment and smiled politely before adding, "Anyway, I have to go. See you." and walked off with Emma, skipping and dragging both me and Kevin out of the cafeteria. Was Mick drunk or something? I was quite puzzled as to why Mick even acknowledged my existence for once. What was his game? I grinned to myself, remembering Eric's face as we got to the library. He could get so jealous sometimes, I rolled my eyes and laughed before beginning to help Emma with her project. I'm just glad that we worked things out between us because I didn't realize until now how much better it was with him in my life.

Chapter 12

Florence:

I was lying there, wondering dramatically why my life was so boring right now. It was Spring break, I was supposed to be out doing stuff with my friends but of course, they were all busy tonight. Charlotte was sick, which explained her absence from school all last week. Kevin was out of town with his Dad and Emma was apparently trapped in her house because it was Holy Saturday and she had very strict, very catholic parents keeping her locked up at home.

Just then, my phone buzzed.

Eric: Hiya Flo, I'm bored and I need something to do. Want to come for a spin in my Porsche.;) I laughed at his final words and texted him back.

Me: Although the offer sounds very tempting, your car is far from a Porsche, so no thanks. My phone beeped instantly after I sent the text.

Eric: It's a good thing that I wasn't asking. I'll pick you up at 10. I grinned at my screen and then sprung up from my bed to get ready after looking at the time, it was 9:46pm. I got undressed out of my pajamas and put on dark ripped jeans and a pink top. I ruffled my untamed hair and decided it was better to just leave it as it was.

After I was done making myself look as presentable as possible, I headed downstairs with my shoes and leather jacket in hand. My dad was sitting down on the couch watch TV so I plopped down beside him and began tying my laces.

"Where are you off to?" he eyed me with curiosity.

"I'm just going out with a friend." I said as I put on my other shoe.

"Who? It's getting late." I wondered whether it would be okay to just tell him who I was going with, I'm sure it would be fine wouldn't it?

"Do you know Eric that lives around the corner from us?" he looked like he was trying to picture his face.

"The Montgomery's boy?" he asked me and I nodded quickly, hearing Eric's horn honking outside now.

"Yeah dad, I'll be fine. I promise." I looked at him with pleading eyes and could tell he was trying to make a decision.

"Sure Florence, just don't be home too late okay?" he said before looking back at the TV again.

"I won't. Bye dad." I said before jumping up and walking out the door.

"See you." I heard him say just before I closed the door behind me.Eric was waiting outside my door in his car. It was getting warmer as the days went on and tonight was pretty warm, he had all of the windows down. I opened the door on the passenger side and hopped in to buckle my seat belt.

"Eric." I said curtly and looked straight ahead.

"Florence." He played along and nodded his head. We both laughed and he began driving.

"So where are we going?" I asked as I put the radio on.

"Wherever you want, I was thinking we could just drive around and stop at an IHOP on the way home, it's kind of our shitty tradition isn't it?" I hit his arm and glared at him.

"It is not shitty, I love pancakes." He chuckled.

"I know, I'm joking Flo. I love pancakes too."We talked and drove for about an hour before we pulled over at the side of the road beside some field that was probably farmland. We got out and looked behind the fence into the big grassland; there were a lot of cows lying around. I leaned my arms on the fence and rested my chin in them as I looked.

"You want to go in?" Eric asked from beside me. I turned to him, the pale moonlight hitting his face. I couldn't help but grin.

"No way. What if we get caught?"

"Are you afraid some farmer is going to chase us right out of here with his rifle or something?" he was smirking now at me.

"Chicken." He said before poking my arm. Little did he know, he was entirely right.

"I am not." I pushed him before getting up on the fence but I had trouble getting over it.

"Little help here Eric." I rolled my eyes because I turned my head and caught him looking at my ass.

"Sure, I was just enjoying the view." He replied, causing me to roll my eyes. He soon helped me get over the fence before doing the same himself.

We were lying down on the field, in the middle of all of the cows when a few of them began piping up and mooing loudly. I giggled at the noise, making a "shh" noise but they didn't listen. Now they we all moving closer to the farmhouse and making even more noise. Eric and I heard a door being slammed open and a floodlight coming on. My eyes widened as I looked at him in disbelief.

"Who's there?" we heard a male voice shout.

"Maybe we should go." Eric was holding in his laughter, we began to sneak away in the direction of the fence but it was still a good bit away from us. We heard the chick-chick of the gun before it was fired from behind us.

Although there was a light on, it was dark where we were so the farmer couldn't see us. We began running until we reached the fence and Eric helped me over. I ran to the car, I could still hear the man's voice coming closer as Eric slammed his car door shut and sped off quickly. We drove for five minutes in silence and pulled in to an IHOP parking lot. He shut off his car and let out a sigh of relief. We turned to each other, I was sure my face was white with panic because his was too. He gave me a 'what just happened' look before the two of us burst out into laughter loudly.

"Oh you should've seen the look on your face Flo." he said between laughter and slapped his knee.

"Me? Have you seen yourself?" I giggled back at him and we both got out of the car. It clicked as he locked it and we made our way to the entrance of the restaurant. He held the door open for me and gestured I go first.

"After you m'lady." He said in a funny voice and went in the door. He followed and we got a small booth. After a waitress came and took our orders and menus, I looked around the empty restaurant. There was no one here except for us and a person sitting at the counter, chatting to the waitress.

"It's kind of empty isn't it?" I asked, still looking around.

"Well it is almost midnight on a Sunday morning. Not many people enjoy eating pancakes at this time." He chuckled.

"I find that hard to believe, who doesn't enjoy eating pancakes at any time?" I said in mock seriousness and stared out the window at the black sky. I looked up to find him smiling widely at me.

"What are you staring at?" I laughed.

"Nothing." He brushed it off as the waitress placed our food down in front of us.We sat there and chatted for a while over our food. Before paying and leaving.

Eric dropped me home a little after one and said he'd see me later. I reached over and placed a kiss on his lips and began to leave but he pulled me back to him so I fell on his lap in front of him. He kissed me again, a little less gentle than the last and I laughed into the kiss. We looked at each other, our foreheads touching.

"Bye." He smirked at me as I got off of him and left the car. He waited until I got in safe to leave. He could be so sweet sometimes, tonight was really fun. I waved him off and shut my door quietly. I saw a light still on in the living room as I tiptoed past. My dad must be still up; it's kind of late for him though. I know that sometimes he waits up until I return to know I'm home safe.

"Florence?" I heard him call sternly. Oh shit, I thought to myself.

Chapter 13

Florence:

"Hey Florence, who are you texting that's more important than talking to me?" Kevin shoved her playfully. We were sitting outside on a small section of grass in the park, eating ice cream and catching up. When Kevin returned from his trip, he decided we should all meet up and have a chat. We were the first to arrive and were now waiting on Emma and Charlotte.

"Okay, okay. Just give me a second." I said, typing the last few words in my message to Eric and putting my phone away in my pocket.

"Thank you." He held up his hands and let out a sigh.

"What the hell is taking them so long? We told them two o'clock not whenever the fuck you feel like." I sniggered at his words.

"I'm sure they'll be here soon. Don't worry." I talked to him like he was a baby and patted his shoulder.

The pair arrived soon enough after and plopped down beside us. We had been talking about their lateness and how our Spring Break went when a familiar voice called my name from behind us.

"Florence." I turned and found a smiling Jake with Skip by his side, wagging his tail and looking at me.

"Hi Jake, how are you?" I stood up and hugged him. "Oh, these are my friends. Jake- Charlotte, Emma and Kevin." I pointed to each of them sitting on the ground.

"Hello there." He said in a friendly tone, "I was just walking Skip and I noticed you over here, thought I would come over and say hi." He smiled at everyone.

"He's so cute, can I pet him?" Charlotte asked Jake.

"Sure." He said and Charlotte got up to her knees and patted Skip. I joined in for a moment as we caught up with each other.

"Well anyway, I better get going. It would've been rude to not say hi."

"Okay, I'll see you Jake." I waved at him.

"Bye, it was nice meeting you all." He addressed my friends and then left. As I sat back down, I could feel all of their eyes on me. When I looked up, Kevin was grinning at me but not saying anything.

"What?" I asked them all.

"Nothing." Emma giggled.

"So that's why you're mind has been somewhere else the past while." Kevin finally said something but his guess was wrong. It wasn't because of Jake, it was because of Eric but I couldn't say that to them all.

"No." I trailed off. I noticed how Charlotte hadn't spoken but was smiling ever so slightly at me, like she knew something else.

"He's hot." Kevin stated. "I can see why you like him."

"I do not!" I denied it because I really didn't see Jake like that. I couldn't deny he was hot but I had Eric.

"He is kind of hot Florence, you have to say." Emma admitted quietly and looked shyly at me.

"That doesn't mean I like him."

"So you do think he's hot?" Kevin laughed.

"What? No! Well yes but, oh whatever." I turned away from a laughing Kevin and Emma, Charlotte had continued to be quiet but laughed lightly at my behaviour. We all sat there for almost the entire day and then made our way home.

On the way down my street, Eric's car drove by slowly and then reversed to crawl slowly beside me as I walked. He rolled down his window and smiled at me.

"Hey there stranger." He said in a funny voice, causing me to chuckle. "I haven't seen you in a while."

"I'm sorry, I'm still trying to recover from my near death experience that I had the last time we went out together." I joked and we both laughed.

"Want a ride?" I was still walking alongside his car and he was still driving at a snail's pace.

"To the end of my street?" I burst into laughter again, I was only three houses away from my front door.

"Well yeah, hop in." he reached over and opened the passenger and I climbed in. We drove for about two seconds and I reached my house. "Well we've finally reached your destination."

"Thanks so much Eric, I couldn't do it without you." I said sarcastically. I looked up to find him grinning wildly at me. "What?" I spoke.

"Nothing." He answered. We sat there looking at each other in silence, I knew I was being weird but I didn't want to go yet. I didn't want to say goodbye just yet but I started wave and open the car door.

"Hey, can I come over tonight?" I stopped myself and turned around.

"Sure, my mom is away again so it's no problem." He had one hand on the steering wheel and the other was leaning on the car seat. He looked genuinely happy right now, we both knew why. His smile reached his bright blue eyes and he spoke again. "I'll wait here while you get your stuff."

I went inside to my find my dad cooking himself supper and listening to the radio.

"Hey kiddo, how are you keeping?" he looked up from the frying pan to me.

"I'm fine dad. Just here to pick up my stuff for tonight, I'm staying in Charlotte's for the last night of my break." When did I get so good at being able to lie to him? I wondered.

"Sounds good, but will you be home early tomorrow? I was going to ask if you wanted to come to the shop."

"Sure dad. I'd love to." I agreed to be home before eleven and then ran upstairs to grab a few things and put them in my over-night bag. After getting everything ready in about two minutes which was good for me, I practically leapt down the stairs and went into the kitchen again to say goodbye to my dad.

"I'll see you tomorrow." He said and I closed my front door, making my way to Eric's car. When we got there we ate and watched Netflix. He sat on the edge of the sofa, with me sprawled out and lying my head on his lap.

"Pass me the Doritos bitch." I held my hand up near his face and waved it, an attempt to annoy him. He smacked it away and continued to text on his phone. "C'mon." I done it again and then pushed his face in different directions.

"Florence. Stop." He tried to sound serious and hold in his laughter but it wouldn't last. He put his phone down and continued to hit my hand away. I covered his face with my hands now.

"C'mon." I said and turned to sit up.

"Stop it!" he laughed, "God you're so frustrating." He breathed out and I crossed my arms and sat beside him, huffing and puffing and trying to throw a pretend tantrum.

"So what?" I asked and he burst into laughter until he snorted which would probably be unattractive to anyone else but it just made me laugh too.

"Shithead." I shoved his shoulder with mine and then he pinned me to the chair. My shirt was riding up and I could feel the soft material on my exposed back as I lay down.

"What did you just call me?" he squinted in mock disgust and then I giggled before he crashed his lips on mine. There was more want in the kiss than I expected and he began to trail soft kisses down my neck as I helped him pull his shirt over his head. My hands skimmed his muscular back and I ran them down to his waist. We were too pre-occupied with our make out session to hear Eric's front door shutting and the footsteps that came along with it. Eric whispered in my ear and I moaned.

"Woah, what the hell?"

Chapter 14

Florence:

"Whoa. What the hell?" We looked up to find Mick looking in awe at the two of us. I covered myself immediately with my hands, Eric moving in front of me too. I looked around and tried to find my top which had been thrown somewhere around the room by Eric.

"Dude, get out now! Cover your eyes." Eric made sure Mick wasn't looking at me. Mick turned around with his back to us and put his hands over his eyes with a roll of the eyes and a huff.

"Okay, okay." He said. We jumped up and tried to find my top. I picked it up from behind the sofa and put it on.

When Mick turned around, my face reddened at his smirk.

"I told you not to come over, I was busy." Eric said angrily. I sat there with my hands on my needs, avoiding any eye contact with the two boys whatsoever.

"Busy with whats-her-face." He said humorously and pointed at me, crossing his arms and leaning on the doorway. "God, I knew it! I knew I was right." he shook his head in disbelief.

"Her name's Florence!" Eric shouted, causing me to look up at him. His nostrils were flared and he was glaring at Mick.

"Whatever man." He threw his arms up in surrender, "I didn't mean to offend your girlfriend." He snickered.

"She's not my girlfriend, this is the first time." He spit out, like I disgusted him. He hated being wrong and I knew this but he didn't have to say it so harshly. His words stung a little but I tried not to show any emotion on my face. I looked down at my hands now.

"Whoa, relax okay? I didn't mean to offend you. Don't worry Florence, I wouldn't mind spending some alone time with you." He winked at me, causing Eric to get up out of his seat and stalk towards him.

"Shut up. Don't talk to her like that."

"You know, you are getting really defensive, considering she isn't even your girlfriend. Are you sure about that Eric? Just wait until I tell the guys about this, they'll flip." He laughed, taunting Eric.

"Don't you dare Mick. You can't tell them about any of this."

"Well then maybe you should start being a bit nicer about all of this. I'm sure Florence wouldn't mind."

"Maybe I should go?" I said quietly and stood up to grab my things, this was getting awkward now.

"No Florence, it's fine." Eric turned to me and spoke softer than he had been to Mick. "Mick was just about to leave." Eric spoke through gritted teeth at his close friend.

"Okay, whatever. If you wish." He put his hands by his side and walked out the door, leaving us in a deafening silence. Eric stood with his back to be for a moment and then turned around.

"Shit, shit, shit." He muttered under his breath as he paced up and down in front of me. He was panicking I was sat down on the sofa, my hands tangled in each others now and tapping my foot. What did I do now? I thought.

"You know, I don't mind leaving. I'll grab my things and walk." I finally spoke.

"No, please, I want you to stay." His plea did sound genuinely but I couldn't forget about the way he was going on and the things he said to Mick.

"Really?" I asked, trying not to let my voice waver. I felt terrible right now. Was this situation really that bad? I thought to myself. He stopped fidgeting and walking to look directly at me.

"What's that supposed to mean?" his eyes closed slightly.

"It means that you look like you need to be alone right now and I don't want to be here with someone who doesn't want my company." I was surprised at my last words, I was never ever that straight with him.

"What makes you think I don't want your company?" he looked slightly taken aback, like he had no clue what I was talking about. Could he not see what he was doing all this time? I had to choose my next words carefully here; I had to decide whether I wanted this argument with him right now or not.

"Nothing. It doesn't matter anymore." I looked down again.

"If I didn't want you here, I wouldn't have asked you to stay." He walked towards me and took me in his arms in a tight grip. "I'm sorry if I made you think otherwise, I really do want you here Flo." His voice was muffled slightly.

"Alright then, I'll stay." I said, hugging him back and then letting go to look up into his bright blue eyes.

"Let's go to bed, it's late." He took my hand and we went upstairs.

We had gotten ready for bed and hopped in. I hadn't realized the time until I looked over at Eric's digital clock on his bedside table that ready 1:02am. I turned away from him, my mind racing with a thousand questions, when I felt his arm wrap around me and pull me closer so our bodies were touching. I felt the warmth of his body and his lips on my cheek before he spoke.

"You okay?" he whispered. I turned around to face him and looked up at his face that was illuminated by the blue light of the moon that had crept in through the window. He looked concerned and too awake to be able to drift off to sleep. I paused for what felt like hours, the room was dead silence, and finally spoke.

"Do I disgust you?" my eyes began to tear up. He looked confused.

"Of course not. I- No." he spoke with finality but his words weren't enough to reassure or comfort me. "What would make you think that?" he asked.

"Nothing, it doesn't matter anymore." I whispered back. He wiped away a tear that had slipped down my cheek and held me closer and kissed my forehead. It did sooth the pain a little but I wasn't convinced and my thoughts were beginning to get the better of the situation now.

Why couldn't I just say what was on my mind? Why did I hold back so much? I needed to stop and have an honest talk with Eric but I just couldn't bring myself to do it. Maybe another time.

Chapter 15

E ric:

"Do I disgust you?" she asked me and I noticed her eyes had become watery. What? Was she serious? How could she not know how absolutely crazy I was about here by now? Because you're trying your very best not to show it Eric. My subconscious but into my conversation with myself. That may have been right but I had my reasons. Maybe I was a chicken, I knew she wouldn't stay for much longer if I kept going on the way I had been but I just couldn't yet.

"Of course not. I- No." I replied, the answer she deserved was on the tip of my lips right now but it never passed them. Instead, I asked her "What would make you think that?" I gulped.

"Nothing, it doesn't matter anymore." That was the second time tonight she had said those words to me and I couldn't help but feel like it actually did matter to her. I wanted to comfort her with words but I wasn't going to be able to quite yet. So I wiped away her fallen tear, held her tight and kissed her forehead.

Flo was such an amazing girl, like no other but that didn't stop me from blabbing my mouth in front of Mick when he walked in and caught us in the act. I would be happy with everyone knowing about us except that that would make the feelings seem more real.

Sometimes when I thought about it, I thought I could love her, but that would be a silly thing to do. Love comes and goes, it didn't permanent and stable which is why I decided to kick it to the curb. I didn't need to love or be loved by anyone, it was tricky and made things messy so this thing that we both had going on was perfect for me, up until a little while ago when I started to really think about it.

Needing to get my mind away from Florence, my thoughts began to tangle up around Mick and what I was going to do now. Would he tell everyone? With my persuasion, I didn't think he would, at least not for a while anyway. Maybe I needed to cause a diversion, make him think that what I said was true. Or maybe you could just tell everyone the truth... The thought made my stomach flutter anxiously, the bad kind too. No, not yet, I couldn't do it.

"What are you doing to me Florence?" I whispered but she was sound asleep, she wasn't snoring but I would have to mention she was tomorrow to tease her. My head said I needed to get her away from her but my heart wouldn't let me. What the hell was I to do now?

Chapter 16

F lorence:

It had been a while since that night at Eric's and what was said was pushed to the back of my mind. I only had two months or so left with Eric before he finished high school for good and went off to college. We hadn't spoken about that yet, nor did I want to either. Thins went on pretty normal, Eric and I went out a lot (even though he seemed a bit more cooler with me than usual), I went out with friends, school was busy, everything was the way it usually was.

One Saturday evening, I texted Eric to ask if he wanted to do something but he took quite a while to reply which was unusual.

Eric: Sorry Flo, I'm busy. I can't.

Hmm, okay then, I thought and called Charlotte.

"Hi." She said when she picked up.

"Hiya, feel like doing anything tonight. I'm bored."

"I'm going out with Evan tonight -but you can come too?" she sounded enthusiastic but god knows I would rather sit here and look at the four walls of my bedroom than go out with my friend and her boyfriend.

"Oh no, it's fine really. I'll find something else to do." I was sorry I asked now.

"No, Evan won't mind. I promise, we're going to the movies. It will be great!" she always seemed so happy and upbeat ever since she and Evan started seeing each other. It was great to see her like that! But I had to decline the offer again, even though Evan was really nice and all.

"I don't want to third wheel."

"Nonsense girl, be ready by nine." She said with finality in her voice before hanging up on me. Third wheeling it is then! I thought.

We went out at nine, just like Charlotte had said. I heard Evan beeping outside my house while I was finishing off getting ready and flew down the stairs, grabbing my things and saying goodbye to my dad before I went on my way.

"Hello Florence. I haven't seen you in a while, where have you been hiding?" Evan was his usual friendly self.

"Under the rock I came from, I really need to start going out more and getting new friends so I can stop third wheeling with you two guys." My comment caused them both to laugh as I shut the back door of the car and we got going.

It wasn't awkward like I thought it would be, Charlotte and Evan didn't seem to mind me being there. We were queuing up for our tickets when I saw a familiar face in the corner of my eye. I turned my head slightly. Is that Eric? I thought to myself. I was right, it was Eric. He was standing there, looking gorgeous in a raglan t-shirt that was tight enough to show off his muscular and athletic frame but not too tight and jeans. His hair was done nicely; like he only got it cut and he seemed to be waiting on someone but who? He checked his watch but didn't look in my direction. I didn't want the others to see him so I decided not to look in his direction.

We eventually got our tickets and snacks and then went inside to find our seats. My eyes searched around for Eric, hoping he hadn't come to the same movie as us but my eyes settled on his familiar face but he couldn't see her in the dark. Her eyes followed him as he walked up the stairs and trailed down to his left hand where he was holding another's.

My heart sank a little in my chest when I realized who it was. It was Chloe.

They both go into their seats just a few rows in front of us. Charlotte and Evan were whispering about some-thing while I stared.

"You alright?" Charlotte shook my shoulder lightly, getting my attention.

"Yeah, of course. I was just in a stare. Sorry."

"Shh, it's about to start." Evan said excitedly and we both chuckled.

The movie was complete torture for me, not because of the bad acting, blood and guts, or the unrealistic fighting scenes. It was because of what was taking place in front of me, just a few seats away from me.

"This is the best part yet." Evan said in a hushed tone to both of us. I nodded, pretending to look but then I looked again at Cloe and Eric, who had been swapping spit for the millionth time tonight. How could he? Because you aren't together Florence, I answered my own question. I felt like such a fool right now but at least no one else knew about it.

I wanted to just be somewhere else, preferably under my covers or the rock I was talking about earlier, so I didn't have to face the embarrassment that no one else knew about. But it was all happening down on row J, things were getting pretty heated pretty quickly too. I didn't need to watch the end of the film, I was watching my own right here, live too.

Another thought that didn't cross my mind at the beginning was how the hell we were supposed to get out of here without bumping into him and Chloe. My stomach lurched; maybe I could sneak out before it ended.

"I need to go Charlotte. I'm sorry, I feel sick." I whispered to her.

"Do you want me to come with you? We can all go and drop you home if you like?" she replied, looking at Evan who was watching the screen intently.

"Oh no, it's fine. I'll call my Dad to pick me up. He won't mind." I smiled weakly at her before standing up and getting out of the aisle, past Evan and Charlotte.

"I'll see you." She said quietly and waved. I waved back and walked quickly down the stairs, making sure to not look anywhere near Eric. He was too busy anyway, whispering in Chloe's ear, to notice me. Once I got out of the cinema, I let out a sigh of relief. Thank the heaven's I got out of there quickly, I thought. But now I had another problem: it was past eleven at night, I was upset, and I had no one to call except my dad who would know something was up.

My eyes teared up at my realization but I patted them away quickly before tears appeared. I eyeballed my phone, wondering what I should do when I remembered someone I had forgotten about. Hopefully he wasn't busy, if he was I would rather walk home than call my father.

I dialed his number, sniffling. Oh no, now I wascrying.

"Hello." My voice wavered as I wiped my eyes.

"Florence? Are you okay?" he sounded concerned. "What happened?"

"Can you pick me up Jake? I was at the movies with Charlotte and her boyfriend and we seen Eric and he was with someone and I didn't know what to do and we went into the movie and I couldn't watch it and-" I was really crying now.

I knew Jake wouldn't be able to understand what I was saying through my sobbing or would he understand why I was upset or who Eric was but I needed to talk to someone. Him being outside of my circle of friends, and not even attending my high school meant it might be safer to tell him about it rather than anyone else I knew.

"Hold on okay? I'll be there in a few minutes. Where exactly are you?"

"The movies." I cried. "Just in town."

"I'm coming okay. I won't be long." He reassured me before hanging up. Why was I being such a drama queen? I thought. But I couldn't stop myself from crying, I couldn't stop myself from feeling hurt.

Just like he said, Jake pulled up a few minutes later at the entrances of the theater, a sad smile on his face when he seen me. He reached over and opened the passenger door to let me in and I walked over and got in. We drove around for a while; he knew not to bring me home yet. I was still kind of crying and upset. He stopped the car in some parking lot after a few minutes and looked directly at me.

"What to tell me what's going on?" he asked, his eyes showing only kindness.

I nodded.

Chapter 17

Florence:

I told Jake everything, from the beginning to the very end. I told him about Eric's offer last year, how he was different with me compared when others were around. I told him about keeping it quiet, about keeping secrets. We never told anyone about each other and how it didn't matter to me for a long time but recently it was getting a little too much to handle. Hell, I even told him about getting drunk at Evan's party and Mick walking in on our make out session.

I was in too much pain to be embarrassed right now, he just hugged me when I told because he didn't know what else to do. After I stayed at Eric's house a while ago, I went to the shop with my Dad and Jake had been there. Since then we had gotten closer but I didn't know why I trusted him with this.

"I just feel so stupid." I said, my voice muffled by his soft hoodie.

"It's okay Florence." He patted my back and released me.

"It's not like he cheated on me or anything, I get that we had no strings. But I can't help feeling hurt, it was awful to have to watch and he didn't even know I was there." He nodded in agreement as I spoke.

"I think that it's understandable for you to be upset, I really do. But I don't know whether Eric will understand, he's never really seen you with another person either but if he really likes you, he would be jealous, and he would feel the way you do right now." He said.

"Should I still talk to him?" I asked, I really didn't know what to do. As much as I wanted to go back to the way it was I couldn't. I knew that there was a chance Eric had been seeing other people all this time but the aching feeling inside of me made me realize that I couldn't and wouldn't have something like this with him anymore. Jake looked at me for moment before speaking again.

"I don't know. I don't want to sound blunt or mean in any way Florence just hear me out." He warned. "But because it was a no strings sort of thing, well, things like that will always happen. If you want to still be with him then you have to get used to that but I don't recommend it, now that you have feelings for him. Things can go bad between you two because it's one-sided."

"I don't have feelings for him." I said quickly. He gave me a knowing look.

"Really? You still think that? Honestly Florence, you have to have realized by now that you at least have some kind of feelings towards him. I know he's a dick and all but you can't help who you fall for as they say." There was a pause for a short while in the car, I was thinking. Thinking about everything that has happened between us two, all of the things I kept from Eric about how I felt and how hurt I was right now. It couldn't mean I had feelings for him could it? Or was I in denial?

We talked about it more in the car. I had stopped crying a while ago and Jake drove me home, noticing it was getting late and he didn't want my dad to be worrying about me. As we neared my house and Jake parked outside, he told me something.

"You know Florence, we don't know each other long but if you ever have a problem don't hesitate to come talk to me okay?" he said before I hugged him tightly.

"Thanks for being there." I smiled weakly at him and then went inside.

That night, I just couldn't sleep. I was tired but my thoughts decided to keep me up. All that occupied my mind at first was Eric and the things he had said to me over the past while that stuck in my mind.

God I missed you.

Just because I don't want to go out with you doesn't mean I don't care about you Flo.

You mean something to me.

You aren't like anyone else and that's what I like about you. I care about you Flo, more than you can ever think.

Were they lies? Maybe he wanted to string me along; I was just someone on the side to keep him busy if he was bored. I just didn't want to think about it like that but I couldn't help myself. I was angry at myself for falling into this trap. Yes, he was the reason I was feeling like this but I was too because I hadn't stopped myself when I had the chance.

It felt like a million things were running through my mind at that moment. I tried to figure out what to do about Eric, did I really want to be with him after what I saw? Sure, I knew that he could see other people and so could I but you don't know what or how you're going to feel when you see them together until it actually happens.

Chloe and Eric. I turned over to one side again and closed my eyes shut, trying to get the image of them two out of my mind but hadn't Eric told me they were just friends that night at the party. Had he only realized he liked her recently or had he been lying all along.

I wondered how and when I would confront him. I was going to look like a fool, I really was. Like some clingy girlfriend that wasn't even his girlfriend. I was the one hurt because I cared about him, and he didn't feel the same way back. What would he even have to say to me? I wish he would just explain his mind games to me, I had had enough of all of this.

I was unsure about a lot of things that night but one thing was certain as I rested my head on my tear stained pillow: I loved Eric.

Chapter 18

Eric:

Chloe's lips were on mine but they weren't the same. They didn't feel as good, they weren't hers. We were in my car and parked outside of her house. She was straddling me and had her hands in my hair. Every time she kissed me I couldn't help but compare it to when I was with Flo. We took a breath and when I looked at her I had this sudden realization of what I was doing. What the hell are you doing here? I thought. I took her gently off of me and said goodnight.

"Don't you want to come in?" she purred in delight. Thank god she hadn't realized there was something wrong.

"Maybe next time, I have to get going."

"Night." She leaned over and kissed me, whispering in my ear before leaving and going into her house. Once she had shut the car door I looked ahead and let out a long breath.

I felt horrible and guilty, it was the worst I've ever felt. I couldn't help but think of Flo and it crushed me. This plan to get my mind off of her wasn't working at all, I needed to give up. I crossed a line tonight, a line I knew from the start not to cross. I just felt the need to get away from Flo, even though she wasn't near me. I was terrified of what I felt for her and my feelings had only grown stronger. I hated myself right now, why was I so stupid?

I would never talk about tonight, I would keep it a secret and never tell. I told myself that from now on, I was going to show Florence just how much I really liked her and how much I wanted to be with her. I was going to put this night behind me, it was a slip-up but there would be no more. The thoughts of all of this scared me too much though. I had a knot in my stomach.

I drove for a while that night to try and escape my thoughts. The music blared and I air brushed off of my face but when I returned home nothing had changed. I wanted to tell Flo how much I was sorry and I realized now what she meant to me but if I told her everything she would be hurt? She would never give me a chance, I knew that for sure. So lying to her is better Eric? My subconscious butted in.

I went to bed with a heavy cloud lurking over me. My eyes were wide open, I couldn't even think about sleeping. I just looked up at the white ceiling and lay with my hands out at each side of my double bed. I wished she was here with me, even if she was sleeping, she could make me feel better. She always did.

I remembered the nights we'd spent here and felt the spot beside me on the bed. God, I was so confused right now, I thought. I didn't know what I was doing, or what I wanted to get out of being around Chloe. I felt like I was going crazy, I tossed and turned all night and still hadn't come to a conclusion.

I had made my decision. I thought that I could leave this behind, I would have to pretend to Flo that it never happened and things would go back to normal. Yes, it did sound better than having to tell her the truth. Although I knew it really wasn't the right thing to do, I couldn't lose her, not now.

Chapter 19

Florence:

Monday morning after my horrible weekend was only worse, if it could be possible. I dragged myself around the corridors and tried my very best to pretend I was okay in front of a very spritely Emma who I had art with first period.

Although art was one of my favorite subjects in school, it still couldn't lift my mood. My classes felt like they would never end and when lunch came around, I was as delighted for a break as I could be. I didn't go to the cafeteria; I didn't want to be around my friends today so I avoided them as much as possible. I went straight to my locker instead, to change my books and then made my way to the bathrooms.

There was no one else in there so I took this time to check out my appearance in the mirror. It really was a sight. My eyes had the darkest circles I'd ever seen under them, they were irritating and itchy from lack of sleep. I was paler than usual too; I noticed a few blemishes on my chin and forehead but was disrupted by the door squeaking open and someone walking in. I turned my head to see who it could be.

Of course, it was none other than Chloe, walking in and standing beside me to fix her make up. She disregarded me for a moment, snobbishly not acknowledging me being here but then we both looked at each other through the mirrors in front of us.

"Hey Florence." She sneered at me, patted some powder on her cheeks. I really wasn't in the mood for her today, of all days. Did she know that I knew? Did she know anything about me? She must because there was no other reason she could know my name. "You know, you look really tired and run down at the moment. Are you sick?" she was using this condescending voice with me that made rage rise within me. She had barely said much to me and I felt like punching her in the face. I never got like this, I knew it was because I was kind of jealous I suppose. Usually I was more laid back and shied away from confrontation with anyone but I guess my bad mood, lack of sleep and pure annoyance of her perfect face had gotten the better of me when I spoke.

"What the hell do you want?" I said angrily, causing her to laugh, and making me want to jump on her even more. I was now considering it, but where was all of this coming from? I was experiencing feelings of rage and anger I had never felt or seen before in myself.

"Some one's touchy today. Any reason?"

"None of your god damn business." She was making me even angrier, and she knew it, she was enjoying this. She absolutely loved it. But I had fallen right into her trap and there I was, standing in the empty bathrooms with her, waiting for her to tell me whatever it was

"I'm guessing it's because you've heard the news then. Don't worry, I'm sure you'll find someone else to bring you to prom." Prom? What was she talking about?

"What?" I asked, I was confused now. She was making me even angrier, and she knew it, she was enjoying this. She absolutely loved it. But I had fallen right into her trap and there I was, standing in the empty bathrooms with her, waiting for her to tell me whatever it was she wanted me to tell me.

"Eric, he's taking me to prom with him. You never were good enough for him anyways." Was she worth it? Was she worth the hassle and strength of lunging right at her in the middle of these bathrooms? I want to hit you so badly, I thought to myself. Whoa Florence, where did that come from? I breathed in heavily, trying to calm myself down. How dare she make a statement like that when she knew next to nothing about me? I laughed bitterly at her.

"Eric mustn't have told you very much about me if you think I care about who he takes to prom with him." I said calmly, because it was the truth. I didn't care much for things like that; I had only gone to one school dance in my years of high school. Emma and Kevin had dragged me to it and after that awful night, I never attended another one. Her expression sunk just a little bit but she smiled again.

"Then why are you so angry?" she asked.

"Because you're pissing me off." I said, grabbing my bag and leaving her in the bathroom on her own. I couldn't stand talking to her for another minute, I would freak out. I stormed off down the halls towards my locker again when I saw Mick turn the corner and begin walking in my direction. Oh great, I thought.

"Hey Florence." He used the same patronizing tone with me as Chloe had just minutes ago in the toilets.

"Glad you remembered my name this time Mick." I said sarcastically, he laughed. Using my combination and opening my locker. He still stood there, looking at me. I threw my eyes to him for a moment and spoke again. "Why are you still here?" I knew I was being rude but I didn't care.

"You're actually very funny when you're angry Florence, I can tell why Eric likes you so much." I glared at him for a moment. "I'm guessing you've heard the news about silly old Eric and his stupid decisions, that's what's got your panties in a twist."

"No actually, it's not." I slammed my locker and looked at him.

"You aren't a good liar Flo." He taunted me.

"Don't call me that." I sighed, I wanted to get out of here, quickly.

"Sorry, is Eric the only one allowed to call you that?"

"Look, if you think I care who Eric takes to prom, I really don't. There's nothing more than what you saw the other night between us. You can tell whoever the hell you want. I don't care anymore." I crossed my arms.

"I already have." The penny dropped, Eric hadn't told Chloe, Mick had. He knew what he was doing, Chloe was the biggest gossiper in the school, and she liked to make people's stories her own too. Evan better, I thought, not only would people know about what Mick saw that night, there would be a much more dramatic twist on it. I couldn't wait to hear about this.

"Why would you tell Chloe?" I asked him, I didn't understand.

"I just thought she should know what she's getting herself into before her and Eric become official." Was he usually this annoying? He smirked at me, like some Sharpay from High School musical that actually thought I gave a crap.

"Official?" I was the one laughing now. Where the fuck was all of this coming from right now? I thought. I was glad I didn't know anyone else like Chloe and Mick. Knew very little about them and had only one conversation with each of them and they were the most irritating people I'd met yet. They obviously cared a lot about what happened in high school. Sure, most people did, but the way I always thought of it was that when you're older, who is going to ask you were you popular or how many buys you dated, or whether you were cheerleader captain or of course, if you went out with the infamous Eric, I could not leave that one out could I? The answer was no one. Once you leave high school your reputation is gone, no one cares.

"Yes, didn't you hear?" he asked me but I just like Chloe, I could not waste any more time communicating with him right now.

"No actually I didn't. And quite frankly, I don't want to hear about it because I couldn't give a crap. Make sure you pass on that message to the biggest mouth in school and yours truly, Eric for me will you Mick?" I patted him on the shoulder, smiling at him. He had a defeated look on his face and I felt like I had won this round but would there be any more? "Thank you." I said before slinging my backpack over my shoulder and walking out of school.

I was now in the same place I had been a couple of weeks ago. Sitting here in the exact spot in the park by the lake, my stomach full with McDonalds and junk food and my face stained with tears. It was hard to explain how I was feeling, it was kind of like a mixture of confusion, anger and sadness. I was confused that I was now seeing Eric in another light, the way most people saw him: the playboy who didn't care. I was angry at Eric for doing all of these things coming out that I had never known about and I was angry at myself for caring. I was sad because I understood now that what Eric and I had was definitely gone, there was no going back and whether Eric would feel the same way I did about it (Which I highly doubted) did not matter, we just weren't meant to go together. I had only seen that now.

Chapter 20

F lorence:

I was lying on my bed listening to music when I heard a knock on my door.

"Come in." I said loudly. The door opened and I was surprised to see Charlotte standing there in front of me.

"Hey." She said quietly as she stepped in and shut the door behind her. "Your dad let me in, I just wanted to see you."

I hadn't spoken to Charlotte, Emma or Kevin properly in a while now. I was too busy trying to calm my racing thoughts and avoiding Eric and his calls and messages. Why was he still trying to talk to me, couldn't he get the hint already?

"Want to sit?" I asked, sitting up and leaning my back against my head board. She walked over to the bed and sat down, mirroring me.

"So how are things?" she asked me, but I wasn't looking at her. I held my knees close to my chest now, and focused on the wall in front of me.

"Fine." I said quietly. I was lying though. I was actually stuck in a rut and I had no one to talk to or ask advice from. There was a silence that filled the room for a few moments before Charlotte spoke again.

"What's Eric done now?" she asked casually, but a hint of concern could be detected from her voice.

"Something he can't fix." I mumbled, surprised at how she found out but too tired to show it. Could Chloe have spread it around already? "How did you know?"

"I've always known Florence, I am your best friend after all."

"Really?" I turned my head to look at her now. She nodded.

"I had a feeling, since well ages ago. But I only put together the pieces fully a few months ago. We were at Evan's party and you were drunk and muttering some nonsense about how much you liked Eric's house. He said he'd take you home, he seemed so protective and concerned about you that when he offered to take you home, well I wasn't sure Florence. But I knew it; I knew you two had something going on and that he'd bring you home safely so I let you two go." I covered my face with my hands in embarrassment.

"Oh god, did I say anything else about it that night?"

"No, don't worry." She laughed. "Evan helped me to put the pieces together, he told me how Eric had been acting weird lately and we both talked about you two."

"I'm sorry I didn't tell you Charlotte, but please, don't tell anyone else. It was supposed to be a secret."

"But why?" she asked, curiosity showing on her face.

"Why?" I gulped. Why? I thought. I tried to come up with an answer.

"Yes, why. It's clear that you two care about each other, so why keep it a secret?"

"I- I don't know. I guess I just went along with it, I didn't care. We were never a couple Charlotte."

"Could've fooled me." She replied. "It's so obvious your feelings' are there, why not act on them?" If I had been having this conversation with Charlotte last weekend, I probably would've cried but I was over that now. I was more angry than upset right now.

"They aren't. I really liked him Charlotte, I did, but I know he doesn't feel the same. Sometimes, I would think he maybe could and recently, well it's been great between us but I haven't been honest with him. I haven't spoken up and said what I wanted to say to him and now everything's messed up. I know now, he never felt the same about me."

"What do you mean? What did he do?" she quizzed me about all of the things that happened between us. I told her everything, just like I had with Jake and it made me feel better as she listened intently. Her brows furrowed at the mention of Chloe and our chat in the bathrooms a few days ago.

"She's just jealous Florence, can't you see?" she replied.

"Of what?" I laughed, she really had nothing to be jealous about.

"That Eric genuinely likes you, you have him wrapped around your finger I bet."

"No." I shook my head, "I don't. I don't want him there either, I'm done with all of this." I said with a lot less finality than I wanted.

"I know that if all of these things with Chloe and what Mick said are true, then Eric really isn't good enough for you. Hooking up with other people is what you signed up for, not an actual relationship. But I think that there is still a chance that those two were lying, you need to ask him first."

"I'm staying away from him from now on. I don't ever want him to make me feel the way I did last weekend again. It was partially my fault too which means I have to be more careful." We talked for a while longer and then Charlotte left.

"Just think about what I said, okay?" she gave me a hug before leaving and held me at arm's length. I nodded but

I knew I wouldn't. I would just leave it and both of us would go on with our lives.

Once she left I was on my own again, lying on my bed listening to music. I had another message from Eric but I didn't bother reading it. I thought about how it might be a little unfair of me to not give Eric a chance to explain to himself but if I was honest, I felt embarrassed about the whole thing now, including my feelings.

I had pushed everything aside that I felt I needed to say to Eric all the way through the months we had spent together. All of these things, these little realizations and insights into what happened, were only coming to me now.

There was this deep sadness and regret with in me that I didn't tell Jake or even Charlotte about. Although a part of me was done with everything and the complications of Eric, there was still a sliver of me remaining that wished he would want me. That he would like me back and that Chloe and Mike were lying to me. I wanted Eric, when I thought about it, I really did but not now.

It had taken too many bad feelings instead of good to realize how deeply I had fallen in love with him over the last few months. I loved our visits to IHOP, our drives, just talking to him made my day even a little bit better. I regretted holding back, and although it was something I would never let pass my lips, I admitted to myself that if I could go back and change things, I would. But I couldn't.

Chapter 21

Florence:

I massaged my temples and leaned against the wall in the hallway. The pumping music was way too loud for me; I was in no mood for a party but I had decided I wanted to get my mind off of things and Charlotte said we should go.

I was waiting upstairs in a queue for the bathrooms, the line was moving slowly and I honestly felt like throwing up right now. My vision was blurry and the hallway felt like it was spinning. I wasn't as drunk as I had gotten the last time we went out but I still felt tipsy and I definitely regretted it. I didn't want to be a burden on Charlotte again so I stopped drinking just a while ago but the effects of the alcohol I already consumed were kicking in.

"Hurry the hell up in there!" someone slammed their fist loudly on the door and soon enough it opened up only to reveal Chloe and some random guy. Her eyes made contact with mine and I just wanted to die. If I was sober I would probably run off, too embarrassed to even look at her because of our conversation last week and how my anger had gotten the better of me but I wasn't sober, so I glared back at her when she looked me up and down. She eventually passed by me and I continued to wait in line.

Once I was finished in the bathroom I went downstairs to find Charlotte again. She was in the kitchen with Evan and they seemed to be having a lot of fun. I didn't want to intrude on their heavy make out session in the corner so as soon as I passed the threshold of the door, I walked back out.

We were at one of Evan's friend's parties, which meant it was also one of Eric's friend's parties too but I hadn't seen much of him. I stole the occasional glance at him from the other side of the room when he wasn't looking but I didn't even think he knew I was here.

I walked out onto the dance-floor after gulping down another drink. I danced straight into the middle of the crowd and moved to the music. I felt someone behind me but didn't look. A pair of hands went to my waist and I moved closer to them, both of us dancing now. He leaned down and kissed my neck briefly. I turned my head to look at him, I noticed the familiar blonde hair and turned to face him now, still dancing. It was Eric.

I felt like I was fighting with myself these past couple of days. One half of me wanted to talk to him, to return his calls and messages and be with him again. But the other side told me to stand my ground, and that he was with Chloe now but didn't she come out of the bathroom with another person that didn't look like Eric at all actually?

"Miss me?" He said flirtatiously. I could smell the hint of alcohol off of his breath and before he could say another word, I grabbed his neck and kissed him hungrily. He kissed me back, with me tangling my hands in his hair and him biting my lip when we stopped for air. He looked at me through his long lashes and grinned.

We danced for what felt like ages, our bodies movies against and with each others. And for a moment everything felt like it was in slow motion, all that mattered to me was standing here, looking up into Eric's eyes. We both stood there: not saying a word, our faces blank. I took in his face, I missed him being so close, I missed his presence and right now, if I wasn't so afraid, I would tell him I loved him but it was no good. I didn't want him to ruin it by telling me that he didn't love me back so I just pretended that he did in my mind. I held his face in my hands and he kissed me again.

Kissing him only made me comprehend how much I actually missed him the past week or so. We were probably both a little drunk at the moment and when we were dancing again and he whispered in my ear that we go back to his house, all I could do was grin back at him and say yes. Because this was what I wanted, I wanted Eric and this was probably the last time I would ever be with him. My drunken mind hadn't thought about everything else, about Chloe or what this meant for the pair of us.

He took my hand and led me out of the crowd. I still hadn't thought about what I was doing and how it could be wrong when we neared his house, or opened his door, or even when we went upstairs. It was only when I woke up the next morning with a pounding headache and Eric wrapped around me did I come to think about my actions.

What the hell have I done? I thought. I had just gotten rid of all of the progress made. Hadn't I only told myself a few days ago that we weren't meant to be together? I was confused and very tired. I began to panic at the thought of Charlotte, I had completely forgotten to tell her where I was going and I think one of the reasons was because I was afraid she would stop me. I didn't even want to check my phone, in case she had left about a million messages and missed calls for me to answer.

I turned my head slightly to see a sleeping Eric with a vice grip of me. The warmth of his body was inviting me to stay but I really couldn't. I heard his light breaths in my ear. He looked so perfect in that moment: his blonde hair disheveled, his pink lips parted slightly. I forced myself not to smile.

I managed to take his arm from around my waist without waking him up. Sighing with relief I was about to move closer to the edge of the bed but he grabbed me again, muttering something in his half asleep state. I tried to release his grip again but he woke up, grinning as soon as he seen me. His sleepy blue eyes looked at me.

"Where are you going?" his grin widened.

"I have to go." I whispered quietly, looking around the room. I really did have to go, I was supposed to be staying away from him wasn't I? The sun hadn't come up yet, it was still in the early hours of the morning.

"Don't go." He groaned, pulling me in closer and squeezed my waist. I could sense his smile as he kissed my forehead. I didn't know what to do, his arms were more than inviting and I really didn't need a lot of convincing but I was starting to get tired of all of this. I needed to go. I definitely needed to go and never end up here again. With the thoughts of what Chloe and Mick told me last week flooding my mind, I managed to get up and grab my things.

"I have to." I said, trying to sound stern as I put on my shoes at the side of the bed.

"Are you okay?" he asked but I was busy finding the rest of my things.

"Mmm." I mumbled once I found everything I began making my way to the door but he had gotten up and grabbed my hand.

"Hey, look at me." He said gently and my eyes moved to his bright eyes. "Are you sure?"

I had to make a choice here, freak out at him for making me so confused or just leave. I was in no state to talk to him right now and my headache was getting worse by the minute. So I just breathed out in annoyance and replied with a "Yes." Before leaving him in his room and leaving his house.

The whole walk home all I kept saying to myself was What the hell have you done Florence. I sick of this, I wanted one thing but couldn't have it. I just wished I had the courage to just tell Eric everything and ask him what the hell was going on between him and Chloe because he acted like he wanted me but he couldn't really could he? It had gone full circle again, I was making my way home in the early hours of the morning from his house, more confused than ever.

Chapter 22

Florence:

Monday morning came quicker than I thought and when my alarm went off early this morning, all I wanted to do was hide under the warmth of my covers and never come back out. I was embarrassed my what I had done during the weekend and the thought of facing Eric and my friends in school was literally killing me.

I had another sleepless night last night and my appearance hadn't changed much from the way it was last week: I was still pale, I still had some blemishes sprinkled over my face and I now had even bigger dark circles under my eyes. I dragged my feet as I walked to my locker, avoiding anyone's eyes and looking at the ground.

My classes all seemed like a blur up until lunch. I couldn't pay attention, I could barely listen and my attempts at doing the work were futile. I sighed as I entered the cafeteria for lunch and found my friends sitting down at a table near the corner of the room. I sat down and said nothing, everyone went quiet and looked at me. I didn't get any lunch, I wasn't in the mood to eat anything right now.

"What?" I asked quietly after I looked up and noticed Kevin, Charlotte and Emma looking at me.

"Nothing." Emma looked away.

"No, not nothing. Florence whatever the hell has got you in this funk I just don't know. But you need to get out of it, you can tell us." He said and I smiled slightly, glad that I had such good friends but I couldn't tell them, not right now.

"Maybe another time." I brushed him off and we all began talking about something else. I was glad to get my mind off of Eric for just a while but my eyes latched onto both him and Chloe who were over the other side of the cafeteria sitting together. I felt horrible and confused. She had her hand on his arm and was laughing at something he said, he smiled but it didn't each his eyes. I turned away quickly in case I was caught.

I was jealous, I knew it. As much as I didn't want to care about Eric, even after everything that has happened, I still did. I couldn't just make my feelings go away. It was hard to except that we had to stop what we were doing, I just couldn't be with him anymore. It was doing no good for me especially at the moment.

I breathed out quietly and closed my eyes for a second. I needed to just stop thinking about him for a while. As much as I tried, my Eric-free thoughts didn't last long, not through lunch, not through art class and not through the entire day. I kept to myself like I had been doing a lot recently and wondered whether I was just being a drama queen or not. Either way I just couldn't help it.

I hadn't actually had a proper conversation with Eric in what felt like a long time but that changed that day after school. I had stayed back a little while longer after my last class had finished, I was behind everyone else and the last person to get to their locker before leaving school. I dragged myself up the hallway and reached my locker.

I was nearly finished switching books around when I heard footsteps and noticed a body standing behind my locker door.

"Hey Flo." It was Eric. I knew his voice and it just so happened to sound very casual and like nothing was wrong. It made me angry, all of my sluggishness had been replaced with rage right now. I slammed my locker shut and looked at him, he looked kind of shocked.

"What exactly do you think I am Eric?" I asked, trying not to grit my teeth. He took a step back, his eyes never leaving my face.

"I-"

"I'm not some string along that you can have whenever you feel like it even though you are close to having a girlfriend. Hooking up with other people and hooking up with me while you're with Chloe is a completely different thing. Do you not feel the slightest bit guilty about what happened the night of the party?" I narrowed my eyes at him.

"I'm not with Chloe, what the hell are you talking about Flo?"

"Oh really?' I said incredulously, I knew I was going to sound like the clingy girl that was just too into a boy who didn't care half as much about her. I was going to seem jealous too, but I just couldn't help it right now. "That's not what she told me, or Mick either."

"Since when would you believe those two over me? If you had a problem with it why not just come to me and ask me?" I knew he was right but that wasn't the only thing I was annoyed about.

"Well I seen you two together too, and you didn't see me." It was beginning to sound like the argument we had at Evan's party a while back except this time he didn't mention jealousy, his face sank at my words and he took a while to finally speak.

"Flo-"

"Don't call me that." He looked hurt by my demand but continued.

"Florence." He said, "What I done was a mistake, you have to hear me out here."

"I don't have to do anything, you can do what you like Eric. We're not together, remember?"

"But-but I'm still sorry, I can explain what happened."

"I don't want you to explain, I don't want to hear it. What you did is something you may or may not have been doing this whole time, I knew that from the very start and that's why I've realized how stupid I was for agreeing to all of this. I can't do it anymore, because it was different in the start. It was like out of sight, out of mind but when I saw you two together, I didn't know what to do." I brushed my fingers through my hair and avoided eye contact with him. "I just can't do it, I can't do this anymore."

"No. No, you don't mean that." He sounded panicked now. His reaction was something I hadn't expected. I hadn't really thought about his reaction actually but I just thought he couldn't care less.

"I do." I nodded weakly and met his eyes this time. I pained me to say it but it needed to be said.

"But- But no, please. I made a mistake Florence. Can we talk about it please?" I had already because walking off but he tried to stop me.

"I'm done talking about it. I know it's unfair of me to just spring all of this, how I feel about everything on you now, and I'm sorry for that. I should have spoken sooner but I just couldn't. I can't keep hooking up with you, I can't be with someone who doesn't want to be with just me. I was cool with it at the start but I'm not anymore. I'm sorry." Everything I said was the truth, he had stopped and let me talk but didn't move when I began walking off again, making my way to the front doors of the school.

Eric didn't follow me, or say another word as I left. A part of me was glad while another wished he would run after me and we could make things better again. I stopped hopping as stopped hoping as soon as I shut my car door and drove off. This was for the best.

Chapter 23

After that day after school with Eric, I was sure of a lot more things than I had been before. I couldn't go back to Eric, whether it be hooking up or a relationship, that was one thing I knew for sure. Another was that I needed to forget about him but it was so damn hard to do. Things like that were always easier said than done. Although I wasn't as reserved as I was before I had talked to Eric, it was still extremely hard to go back to how I had been before, when I was more care-free.

I hadn't talked to Eric since that day. When we saw each other, it was hard to not look away. The embarrassment of it all had died down but I could still sense it sometimes, especially whenever I saw him or Chloe, or even Mick.

Going every day without someone you loved was hard. It wasn't like how they said it was in books and films, it was a hell of a lot worse. Although there was no cliché aching going on in my chest where my heart was, I missed him so much. I had adapted and gotten to use to having him around every day. We may not have seen each other in person but we would at least talk most days.

I tried to go back to the time when everything was normal in my head, but it hadn't been normal in a while. I remembered our visits to IHOP, and that night when we ran away from the angry farmer who was chasing us. I remembered just being in his arms, I remembered how he would squeeze me when we hugged and I remembered our kisses. I had a collection of memories since the first time both Eric and I had met; they were only beginning to surface now, after we were done.

As much as my friends asked me out places, I had to decline their many offers. They knew something was up with me, they mentioned it quite a bit but I wasn't ready to talk to them. Charlotte knew about Eric but she didn't know half of what was going on in my head. As much as they all were just trying to help, it wasn't working. I wondered when it had gotten so hard to go on without one person in your life, how had I not seen it coming: how much I cared about Eric. I was foolish, and now I was going on like some girl in a soppy romance film. It wasn't what I wanted, but it was hard to change.

I was sitting in my living room, watching TV, one Saturday night when I heard the doorbell ringing. I hoped it wasn't Emma or Kevin, as bad as that sounded, I couldn't deal with them tonight. I had already said no to their invitation to Emma's house but it wouldn't surprise me if they turned up at my door anyway. My dad was out of town for tonight so it couldn't have been him either.O nce I walked out into my hallway and opened the door, I immediately froze.

Eric.

He had a painful expression on his face, like he was a mixture of sadness and even more sadness. His hair was messed up and he was frowning. His appearance brought tears to my eyes.

"What?" I croaked out, not able to speak properly.

"Can I come in?" he shifted from one foot to the other on the threshold for a moment and I hesitated. "I just want to talk." He added and I opened the door fully, allowing him to come in. He followed me into the sitting room and sat down.

I sat down on the sofa opposite him, wanting and needing to keep my distance as much as possible throughout this encounter.

"Talk." I finally said.

"I miss you Florence." He remembered to call me by my full name and I was glad of it but I didn't know what to say. Should I just tell the truth or not?

"And I miss you too but whatever we had is done, I can't put myself through anything like that with you again." I looked down at my hands that were resting on my lap.

"What if we didn't go back to how we were? What if we became a proper couple this time?"

"No." I spoke again, I was a lot more angry at his words than I expected. "It took you this long to actually ask me that? Do you know how long we've been hooking up?"

"We could try-"

"No, I told you already. I don't want it now, it's too late. You don't even want it do you Eric? You just don't want this to stop because you've become too used to me and you think I'm easy or something." His jaw clenched at my words.

"Of course not! No, I don't think you're easy at all. Why would you even think that?"

"You haven't made me think otherwise."

"If you don't want a relationship what do you want? Please Florence, I'm willing to do anything."

"Nothing. Not anymore." I said with finality in my voice. I stood up and gestured for him to leave but he only walked closer to my and stayed in the same spot. "I want you to go now, there's nothing else to talk about."

"There is. I haven't said half of what I came here to say."

"I don't want you to tell me anything else, don't hurt me anymore than you have already." He looked even more now by my words. He didn't speak though, just walked slowly past me and to the door. That was when I chose to speak, to say something that continued to play on my mind ever since we first met each other. "You know, all I ever wanted was for you to just look at me. To just acknowledge that I was even there, that I existed when someone else was around." I could feel the tears forming in my eyes now and he noticed this, he moved a step closer only for me to take another back.

"I'm sorry." He gulped and I could see his Adam's apple bobbing up and down.

"You can't just be hot and cold whenever you want Eric. Do you know how many times you've pushed me away since this all began?" I was crying now, I could feel my tears running down my cheeks. I didn't even know why I was so upset; I guess I was finally saying what I had to say. "A hell of a lot, but I still kept talking to you. You make me feel so many things Eric, both good and bad and I don't want that anymore." He was wrapping his arms around me now in a warm and comforting embrace. I inhaled his smell, remembering how much I missed him but this was how it was supposed to be: whether I missed him or not, we needed to stop this. I think I was afraid that night, I think I was always afraid. Although Eric was the one with the commitment issues, I couldn't help but get this nervousness in my stomach when I thought about how much I cared for him.

"Shh. It's okay." He soothed me, rubbing his hands up and down my back gently. He kissed my forehead and I looked up from his hoodie to meet his eyes.

"We just can't do this anymore." I said quietly, he nodded slowly after a minute or two in understanding.

"Okay." He said painfully, squeezing me tighter. I felt like he would never let me go and in that moment, I didn't want him to. But it was soon over and he pulled away with slowness, like he didn't want to but I didn't know for sure. I pursed my lips and looked at his shoulder, avoiding eye contact until he tilted my chin up towards him. His lips brushed off of mine and I kissed him back but it was only for a moment. Once he let go he made his way to the door.

"Goodbye Florence." He muttered.

"Goodbye." I replied but he was already out the door and gone.

Chapter 24

"Florence, just talk to us please." Kevin said seriously but I was avoiding his eyes, and the other two pairs that stood on either side of him. I was looking at the dark green grass beneath me where I sat. It was a warm and clammy day today, which was usual for us coming into the summer months. I had come out here to get some peace and avoid my friends like I have been doing for the past couple of days. I knew that I was starting to gradually come to terms with everything and they had given me the space I needed until now.

It was lunch time but I didn't eat any, Emma had brought her usual packed cucumber sandwich but had yet to open it while the other two didn't have anything with them. We were just outside the school cafeteria, there were a few tables outside for people to sit at and eat when the weather was nicer but I decided, like a lot of people, to just sit on the ground.

The three had already taken seats beside me, with Emma and Kevin sitting Indian style and Charlotte kneeling down. I was hugging my knees and closed my books that were in front of me to finally talk to them. It wasn't fair to keep pushing them away and not talk to them without giving them a reason.

"You haven't been yourself the past few weeks, we need to know if everything is okay Florence." Emma said, she used this serious voice too, which was strange for the care-free Emma. I nodded weakly and then looked up at all of them.

"I'm sorry I haven't been talking to you all, that wasn't fair." I finally said.

"Don't worry about us, just tell us what's the matter. It feels like we've... lost you somehow. You're so distant and quiet lately."

"I-I just, I had something going on but it's okay now." What I was saying wasn't a lie, I was getting over it now. It was getting better.

"You know you can tell us anything, don't you Florence?" Kevin gave me a small smile and with that, I told them about Eric. I didn't go into as much detail as I had with Jake, I didn't feel like talking about Eric anymore. It would make me think about him even more and I couldn't have that. When I was done, the three hugged me.

"I'm glad you sorted everything out Florence." Charlotte said to me as she wrapped her arms around me in a loose hug.

"You can't tell anyone, please. I just want to get over it now, I'm done." I said to Kevin and Emma more so than Charlotte, because she already knew and kept my secret. The two nodded in agreement.

"So you don't want to talk about it anymore?" Kevin asked.

"No, I don't."

"So you're okay?" he added and I nodded in agreement.

"So we're going to all go back to normal now?"

"Yes Kevin!" I said in mock exasperation and he smiled.

"I'm just checking." He held his hands up and we all laughed.

"Now can we talk about something else?" I asked and just like that, we all began chatting like nothing had happened. I didn't know whether stopping myself from thinking about Eric too much was a good thing or not.

I wondered was I brushing things under the carpet but even if I was, I was coping okay now. It was better this way. I knew for sure, both Eric and I were better off not together but when I had imagined it in my head before that night he showed up at my house, well, it wouldn't have felt the way it does now. I feel numb, in a sense, like something is missing and it is: Eric. I convinced myself it would go away after a while. I did love him after all-it wasn't going to be easy, and it would take time. At least now I had something to feel good about now: I was slowly getting back to my old self and I had patched things up with my friends.

My father sat down at the table across from me at dinner that night and just like my friends had done a few hours previously, talked to me about how I was behaving the past while. He was so concerned about me, and I felt guilty because of that. I told him how I was sorry to worry him and that everything was fine now, I was just having trouble with a friend.

"It wasn't that boy I always see you with was it Florence? Anne Montgomery's boy from around the corner?" he had asked me. His words startled me for a minute but I quickly regained my voice. I told him that actually it was, we had become friends but now, we weren't anymore. He had nodded and got back to eating his dinner.

Technically, I wasn't lying to him about Eric, we were friends after all weren't we? Well, kind of. Friends hung out together, friends made each other laugh, friends were always there for each other and made them feel better, which was what Eric had done for me for so long. Friends don't hook up casually though, friends don't stick their tongues down each other's throats either, they also weren't supposed to love the other in that kind of way now were they Florence? I thought to myself before rolling my eyes. Oh shut up, I said defensively, realising I was getting a little weird and stopped talking to myself in my head.

But after a day full of talking and opening up, I felt better than expected. There was a weight lifted off of my shoulders, most of it actually, except there was just one little big still hanging on. A part I knew would probably not go away any time soon.

I crawled into bed that night and let out a long sigh of relief. The covers were cool against my skin, I relaxed into my soft mattress, it would be easy enough for me to slip off into a deep sleep from such a tiring day but just then, my phone buzzed from my nightstand. I reached over to read the message and my eyes widened in shock. Please, not him, I thought, anyone else but him. But it was him, it was Eric and once I read the text, I immediately knew I wouldn't be getting much sleep tonight. My mind began to race and my eyes watered as I looked at the now blurry screen.

Eric: I miss you Flo.

Epilogue

E ric:

I saw her standing there; her eyes were in the shape of big circles. She rustled her messy hair with one hand, holding a cup in the other. She didn't know what to do; I could tell by the way she was fidgeting and looking around.

I spent some time deciding whether to go over to her that night. At the time I was really unsure, my feet took me there before I had enough time to rethink it and looking back, I was glad. Once I was there, I was nervous to talk to her so I just dove right in.

"Hey Florence." I waved and as soon as I had moved my hands, I cursed myself for doing so. I looked so stupid right now!

"Hey." Was all she said, quietly at that too. She took a double take at me and then asked me a question I was asked a lot recently. I knew she was going to ask me soon enough. "What happened to your face?" I looked away from her, not wanting to answer. I had done a lot of stupid shit in my years of high school. One of those was getting into fights, it wasn't something that happened a lot but she helped me sort of well, overcome it when I met her. I learned to talk to her instead; I remember back to the first few months we had met, I just thought she was so amazing. I still did. I wished we hadn't become what we were now. I had pushed her away, didn't talk to her or open up as much in the last few months and I realised that only a little while ago, it was one of those days when all I could think about was Flo. I had those days a lot lately. I had finally got the words to speak.

"I was in a fight." I said, breathing in and out once before I added another crucial detail. "With Mick." She looked kind of shocked and I wasn't surprised. I hadn't told her much lately, which meant I hadn't talked to her about how I had grown to dislike one of my best friends since I was younger.

"What? Why?"

"He's a dumbass that's why." I tried not to sound angry but I had failed and I knew it. "And a liar."

"I don't understand?" she said, and why would she? Florence might of thought she knew a lot, but she had no idea what was going on in my head or in my life recently. It wasn't her fault either, but it was too late to start opening up and telling the truth now so I decided to let her think what she wanted to think.

"He got involved in something that wasn't his business, I mean, telling you I was with Chloe? He didn't even know what he was talking about."

"So you bet him up because he told me something I already kind of knew?" she narrowed her eyes at me and I knew she was starting to get annoyed.

"You don't even know what happened Florence? God, I'm not with Chloe, in any shape or form." I breathed out.

"I don't care, whether you are or not isn't any of my business. It never was either." She snapped. Her words made me think, made me finally push myself to say something else I had been keeping locked inside after a lot of time reflecting on our situation.

"You know, I'm sorry Florence. We shouldn't have kept us a secret. I know it was unfair of me to expect you to keep us from everyone." As soon as the words left my mouth, I was glad I said it. I was something that needed to be said, I needed her to just know that I was sorry.

"No." She looked up at me with her big round eyes and continued. "I'm sorry, it was unfair of me to not say what I wanted to say to you. I was being cowardly not telling you how I felt about some things." What the hell was she apologizing for? I felt even worse now than before. I was the coward. I was the one that didn't want to tell her or anyone else about my true feelings for her. I was crazy about her, and keeping it to myself was my way of dealing with it. But liking someone with such intensity isn't something bad, it wasn't the type of thing that needed to be dealt with either, even though I did think it was. I knew that now.

"If you really do like Chloe, you should go for it, you should just go to prom with her or whatever too. You don't need to deny anything anymore, we aren't a thing and I'm cool." She was fidgeting again and this was my time to make a decision. Did I let her go or tell her everything? She deserved a lot better than me, I knew it all along. I knew that one day, after a long time of not letting her in and pushing her away, being hot and cold with her, that she would stop knocking and now here it was. It was better for her if we just stopped this all. She told me not to hurt her anymore and so I had made up my mind.

"Yeah, I know." I said meekly, but I wanted to say everything and anything else right now. It was just killing me but it was for the best wasn't it? I heard Charlotte calling her name and she immediately turned her head. This pause, this was my chance to just tell her absolutely everything, or make a start at it at least.

"I-"

"I better go. Well, bye Eric." Her words stopped he as she turned to leave.

"Bye." Was all I could reply with. I wanted reach out and touch her, grab her hand and stop her from leaving and ending the conversation. I wanted to turn her around and just let everything I had been keeping locked up in my mind spill out of my mouth with so much force that it knocked her back a little. I wanted her to just forgive me and let us just get back to what we were like in the beginning except this time better, this time we would be official and normal and just perfect because I would be with her.

But I didn't. I just stood there. Froze in my spot, unable to move, my mouth open, ready to go but no words left it. I realized one thing as I watched her retrieving back walk away from me for the last time, it was something I had been trying not to let myself say. It was something I had been trying to convince myself that wasn't true. But now, I just couldn't help it, I knew for sure: I loved her.

Florence:

Sometimes, I felt gloomy but other times, I was perfectly okay. I was getting over Eric, I could just tell and I was so glad. I hadn't talked to him in what felt like months, but it was only weeks. The night he sent me that message, I simply put my phone down and turned over to go asleep, although I had trouble doing so.

So it had been weeks, week's since he had been stood there in front of me, asking me what I wanted, that he would do anything. It had been weeks since I actually got a good close look at him. It had been weeks since I had heard his voice. Until now.

I was standing awkwardly in Evan's living room, holding a red plastic cup in my hand, looking around for Charlotte who had left me in here alone with a few of Evan's close friends. It was coming into the last few days in school and it was his birthday but he wasn't having a huge party like the one a few months ago, just quiet, casual drinks. He was saving the big party for graduation in a few days. There were only a handful of people here. This time I was able to hear myself think, the music was on low, sort of in the background.

"Hey Florence." He gave me a small wave and without thinking, I waved back and replied.

"Hey." I couldn't help but notice his faded black eye and busted bottom lip. His hair was dishevelled looking, his hands were in his pockets and he was looking right at me with his illuminating blue eyes. "What happened to your face?" I blurted out, not knowing what else to say. My curiosity had gotten the better of me. He looked away now, putting a hand on the back of his neck and shifting from one foot to the other.

"I was in a fight." Was all he said, not looking at me. He wasn't in a lot of fights, I knew that for sure but when I had only met him, he had one or two. I think it was all of the pent up anger he had at the time but he soon calmed down. "With Mick." He added and my eyes widened slightly.

"What? Why?" I was surprised, I mean Mick? They were like best friends.

"He's a dumbass that's why." He said lowly. anger evident in his voice. "And a liar."

"I don't understand?" I furrowed my brows in confusion.

"He got involved in something that wasn't his business, I mean, telling you I was with Chloe? He didn't even know what he was talking about."

"So you bet him up because he told me something I already kind of knew?" I was trying to not let my annoyance come through in my voice.

"You don't even know what happened Florence? God, I'm not with Chloe, in any shape or form." He said in exasperation.

"I don't care, whether you are or not isn't any of my business. It never was either." My tone was clipped now and I looked away from him. I didn't want an argument, I wanted to just get on with it, and not have to spend more time than usual thinking about Eric. He hadn't said anything at all so I looked at him and noticed the sad look on his face.

"You know, I'm sorry Florence. We shouldn't have kept us a secret. I know it was unfair of me to expect you to keep us from everyone."

"No." I looked up from my drink to meet his eyes. "I'm sorry, it was unfair of me to not say what I wanted to say to you. I was being cowardly not telling you how I felt about some things." His features formed into a pained expression at my words but he didn't speak. There was a pause again so I continued speaking, something that needed to be said. "If you really do like Chloe, you should go for it, you should just go to prom with her or whatever too. You don't need to deny anything anymore, we aren't a thing and I'm cool." I ran my fingers around the rim of the plastic cup and only glanced up at him when I was done talking. He closed his eyes and let out a breath before speaking.

"Yeah, I know." He said quietly, nodding his head.

"Florence!" I heard Charlotte call and I turned my head to see her in the kitchen waving for me to come over.

"I–"

"I better go. Well, bye Eric." And just like we had started the conversation, I waved awkwardly at him and made my way to leave.

"Bye." He said, giving me a sad smile. I saw him waving back in the corner of my eye just before I turned around to go over to Charlotte.

And that was the last time I talked to Eric Montgomery. He graduated and they all had a great time at Evan's party, or so I heard. I was invited but I didn't go, I wasn't in the mod that night. Instead, I decided to not mope around in my house all night, I chose to go out with Kevin and Emma. Eric went to prom but he didn't bring anyone. As far as I knew, Mick and Eric hadn't spoken since they had that fight, not at prom or graduation or anything.

Eric left for college that summer, to do Sports Science at Farebrooke University. I didn't see him again, and avoided it at all costs if he ever came home to visit or was in town. I didn't want to think about him anymore, I wanted to put my head down and do well in school to get into a good college. But when I did, I couldn't help but feel like a part of me hadn't recovered from not seeing him again. It was like when someone went away for a while and you were waiting for them to come home to see you again except I was left waiting.

I had given Eric a tiny piece of my heart and even if he didn't know it or want to give it back, I just couldn't take it from him. We weren't meant to be, we were just two teenagers who were having fun at the time, who didn't care or think about what we were doing. It was an experience but an experience only. Even when I think about it now, I never regret it. I just couldn't.